Property of Lizzie McGuire

The Orchids and Gumbo Poker Club

Book report!
English Class!
Assigned by Mr. Dig.
Due next week!

The Orchids and Gumbo Poker Club

By *Magnolia Praline*

Manuscript "restored" by Alice Alfonsi
Inspired by the Lizzie McGuire series
created by Terri Minsky
From the episode written by Douglas Tuber & Tim Maile

New York

For more information address Disney Press, 114 Fifth Avenue, New York, New York 10011-5690.

Printed in the United States of America

First Edition
1 3 5 7 9 10 8 6 4 2

Library of Congress Catalog Card Number on file

ISBN: 0-7868-4646-1

Cover design by JOE BORZETTA
Book design by ARLENE SCHLEIFER GOLDBERG
Illustrations by ALFRED GIULIANI

For more Disney Press fun, visit www.disneybooks.com

Contents

Introduction

By Persimmon Pursniketi, Ph.D.
PROFESSOR OF LITERATURE
L'École Douteuse

PUBLISHED IN THE EARLY 1950S, *The Orchids and Gumbo Poker Club* was dismissed by critics as an innocent bit of syrupy froth.

"This slight, sentimental novella is nothing more than a cloying spoonful of rock candy. Not only should you not expect a full meal," wrote *The Tuesday Afternoon Post*, "you should take good care to leave the bathroom door wide open—because the need to regurgitate may come over you at any moment."

Whoa! That is way harsh!

Other critics weren't so kind. "The writing

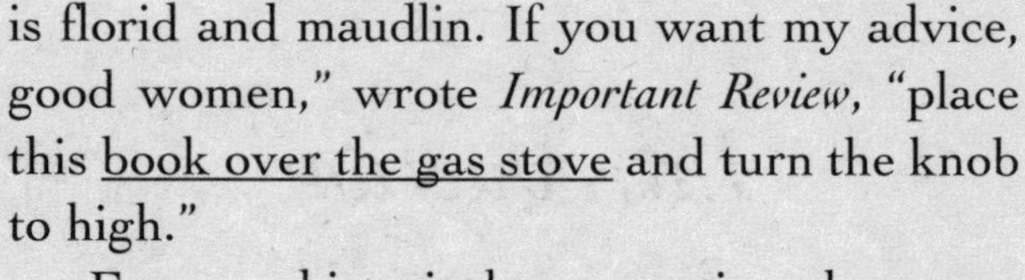

is florid and maudlin. If you want my advice, good women," wrote *Important Review*, "place this book over the gas stove and turn the knob to high."

Uhm—isn't that, like, against the fire code or something?

From a historical perspective, however, readers across America did not give a fig what the critics of that time had to say. Women especially embraced the book as a touching tale of the heart. Copies of the novella were given from mother to daughter at Sweet Sixteens, high school graduations, and, of course, weddings.

Unlike *Peyton Place*—a similarly criticized novel of the '50s, which became a blockbuster best seller of its time, spawned the first prime-time soap opera, and is now considered by many to be a literary classic—*The Orchids and Gumbo Poker Club* fell out of fashion with the passing decades. That is, until I stumbled upon a copy of the out-of-print novella. After bringing it to the attention of the publishing community, this lost classic was swiftly placed back into print.

Note to self: ask Gammy McGuire if this Peyton Place thing was as good as All My Children.

Now a new generation of readers has discovered the charm of this little tale—the story

A mother and a daughter? Guess the book's about being told to clean your room about a zillion times a day. . . .

of a mother and a daughter, of social climbing, of friendship and love. Scholars, too, are taking a closer look.

Social climbing? What? Like Kate's making cheerleader? (Which was totally bogus.)

"The flowery passages are an extension of the subtext of feminine mystique represented in the archetypes themselves," wrote Professor C. Au Lait in her new book, *A Feminist Reading of The Orchids and Gumbo Poker Club*.

Ex-squeeze me? Mr. Dig? Help!?

In the professor's view, this novella, through its young protagonist, provides a pattern of one's relationship to the world as a Jungian extension of the subconscious dream realm.

HUh????. . . .

Part fairy tale, part love story, part melodrama, it transports us likewise away—and yet there is a familiarity, too, as there should be in any fiction considered to be a universal classic.

We see in these beloved characters the people in our own lives. We see our own secret hopes and fears, our own attempts to climb the social ladder, to be close forever to our mothers.

Secret fears? Like being forced to wear a dorky unicorn sweater for your yearbook photo? Been there, done that.

To quote myself from my own recently published *Orchids and Gumbo: A Critical Study*, "The appeal and also the primary significance

Every time I "attempt to climb the social ladder," I miss a rung and end up falling!

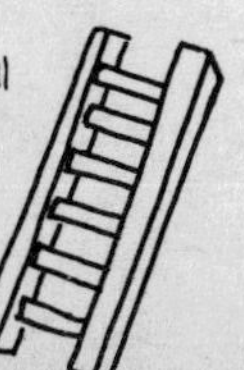

of *The Orchids and Gumbo Poker Club* lies in its conveyance of a narrative that mothers and daughters have been living for generations, and will, no doubt, continue to live for years to come."

Ummm—right. Sure. What-ever.

Enjoy!

"Years to come"? Excuse me? Does she, like, have a crystal ball or something?

Okay, since this was assigned by Mr. D, enjoyment is totally not likely!

Chapter 1
Birthday Girl

DEFINING MOMENTS. THEY COME and go in our lives like streetcars and summer breezes. Like the sweet subtle blush on a honeysuckle blossom—here for the most fleeting of instants . . . then gone again. Do we pick these moments? Or do they pick us?

My defining moments definitely pick me. . . . Like running into locker doors and tripping with cafeteria trays . . . usually when Ethan Craft's around. . . .

Darcy Lou Beignet's very first defining moment took place on the day she turned six, and her three aunts came to help her celebrate.

When I turned six, my big defining moment was pinning the tail on the donkey. And genius me— I pinned the thing to its ear.

Now, these three aunts weren't really Darcy's aunts. But they might as well have been. For they'd been closer than sisters to her mama, Tallulah, since all four of them were

That house sounds so romantic. I wish we had a veranda. Sigh. (Scratch that—I just looked up the word, and it's just a big porch with a roof. We've got a front porch and a deck out back, so those sort of count, right?)

little girls themselves, growing up together alongside those slow-moving waterways, known in Louisiana as the bayous.

"Darcy Lou!" called her mother when the three aunts arrived at the old Beignet house, a well-built home with a wide veranda and great moss-draped oaks. "Sweet potato!"

In her Sunday-best dress of royal purple, six-year-old Darcy Lou came out to the dining room, kissed all of her aunts, and then took the seat at the head of the big mahogany table, as she was told.

This was the very same table where every Saturday afternoon Darcy Lou's mama and aunts played *bourré*—a type of poker they'd learned from their own Cajun mothers, offspring of the French Canadians who'd first settled in Southern Louisiana back in the 1700s.

Hey, my mom probably knows this card game. After all, she worked her way through grad school dealing cards on a riverboat. Guess I never thought about it before, but my mom is pretty cool . . . I mean, for a mom. . . .

Bourré came from the French word *bourrer,* which meant "to stuff"—because this is what a player had to do when she lost. She had to "stuff" the gambling pot with loot. Something every one of the aunts took turns doing from week to week. But never Darcy's own mama,

because Tallulah, the aunts said, was very lucky at cards (and unlucky in love, poor dear).

Tante Maribelle approached the birthday girl first. Maribelle was the most elegant and serious of the four friends because she'd been educated by nuns at a convent school. After that, Maribelle had worked as a nanny for some of the best families in the nearby city of New Orleans. And now, although she'd moved back to their little community of Bayou Le Blanc, she still worked in the city—as a guest instructor at Miss Charlotte's Ballet, Tap, and Charm School.

"Today, Darcy Lou, you are Countess of Jewels!" declared elegant *Tante* Maribelle. "Because you have eyes like blue sapphires and a will as strong as diamonds." And with that, she hung green, gold, and purple beads from last year's Mardi Gras around Darcy Lou's neck.

Tante Jo-Jo was next. She was the plumpest and jolliest of the four women. *Tante* Jo-Jo baked and sewed like a dream, selling her fruit pies and seamstress services to the best bakeries and dress shops on Canal Street.

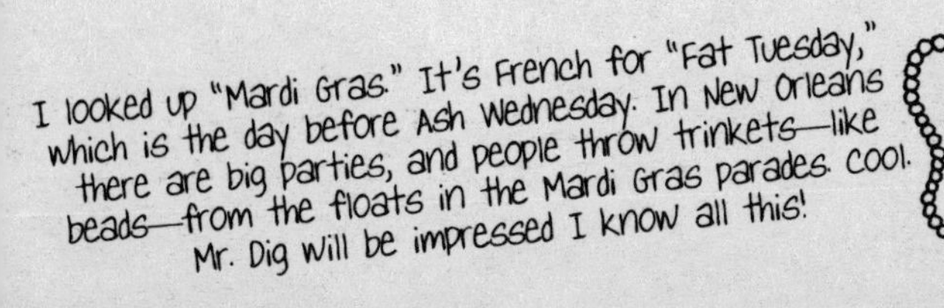

"Today, Darcy Lou, you are Duchess of Gumbo!" declared jolly *Tante* Jo-Jo. "Because you have nature and love around you and that special mix of ingredients that will make you wise and good." Then she presented Darcy Lou with a big pot of seafood gumbo and a fresh sweet potato pie.

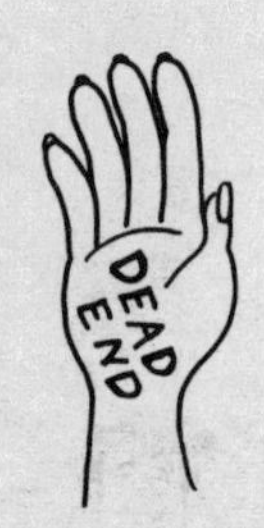

One time Miranda read my palm during lunch period. She said I had a really short lifeline—but then she realized half of it was hidden under a smudge of peanut butter.

Tante Dalphia stepped up after that. She was the craziest of the four women. She lived in the city's French Quarter where she read palms and sold voodoo potions and Cajun remedies to some of the richest women in the city's Garden District.

"Today, Darcy Lou, you are Princess of Cards!" cried crazy *Tante* Dalphia. "Because you will one day learn the powerful and mysterious ways of all women." And with that, she placed a crown of playing cards on Darcy Lou's head of yellow curls.

I wonder if my mom knows the "powerful and mysterious ways of all women"— Note to self: ask!

Next, it was Tallulah's turn to give her daughter something. Darcy Lou's mama was the loveliest and kindest mother a girl could ever have. In fact, her heart was so warm, her smile so kind, and her golden hair so luminous that everyone in Bayou Le Blanc said plants

Awwww . . . that is so adorable. It's how I feel about my mom, too. . . .

reached up through the earth faster and bloomed more sweetly because they mistook Tallulah for the sun itself.

"Tallulah could plant an iron kettle and it'd sprout leaves," *Tante* Dalphia once said.

And so it was. Darcy Lou's mother grew the most beautiful orchids in all of Louisiana. And that's why she made her living selling corsages to the best florist shops in New Orleans, something she was forced to do ever since Darcy's grandfather—the man who'd built the great old Beignet house—had taken ill and could no longer work.

I looked up "corsage." It's not French or anything. It's just a small arrangement of flowers that girls were given by their dates to wear on their dress or in their hair. I dunno. With my luck, if my date ever gave me a corsage, I'd probably end up luring a family of hornets into the junior prom with me.

"Today, my sweet potato, you are Queen of Orchids," declared Darcy Lou's mother. "Because you are God's own orchid child, prettier than any garden flower I could ever grow."

She presented her daughter with a small wooden stick, pulled from her very own orchid garden and wrapped in a ribbon of royal purple.

Then jolly *Tante* Jo-Jo sank six birthday candles into her sweet potato pie, elegant *Tante* Maribelle lit the six candles, and crazy

Tante Dalphia borrowed Darcy's "magic" garden wand to conduct the assembled members of the Orchids and Gumbo Poker Club in an off-key rendition of "Happy Birthday to You."

"Off-key," eh? My twerpy little brother, Matt, must be part of the chorus then. You should hear him sing Christmas carols. Yeesh. He'd drive the dog out of the house—um, if we had a dog!

"Now, take a deep breath, sweet potato," said Tallulah, "and blow hard as a Gulf-borne hurricane!"

Darcy Lou blew. And *Tante* Dalphia, in that crazy gypsy way of hers, waggled her bejeweled fingers and chanted: "Make a wish, make a wish, while the smoke's still here, and it'll take your wish to heaven, dear!"

That's when it happened—Darcy Lou's first defining moment. Watching the wisps of pearl-colored smoke curl toward the ceiling, the little girl declared—

"I wish I knew my daddy!"

Little Darcy Lou didn't know why such a simple wish would make her mama's pretty ivory skin blanch white as a plantation ghost. But Tallulah's three best friends in the whole world knew. And when they saw tears welling up in poor Tallulah's eyes, they quickly made Darcy Lou's wish come true—

"Your daddy!" cried *Tante* Dalphia. "Why,

dear, don't you know? Your daddy, he was a . . . knight."

"A knight?" asked little Darcy Lou.

"Why, yes!" jolly *Tante* Jo-Jo exclaimed. "Just like in those stories your mama reads to you at bedtime."

"In shining armor?" asked the six-year-old.

"Oh, yes," elegant *Tante* Maribelle said, all serious. "And he sat at King Arthur's round table."

"And killed dragons," said crazy *Tante* Dalphia.

"Dragons!" exclaimed Darcy Lou.

"Oh, yeah!" said jolly *Tante* Jo-Jo. "Hundreds and hundreds! That's why folks 'round here put shrimp and crab in their gumbo. There's no more dragon meat. Your daddy killed them all!"

And for the rest of the year, every Saturday afternoon, when her mama's four best friends came over to play bayou poker, Darcy Lou would hear stories of her father the knight, who killed dragons and saved princesses, and won tournaments all over the great state of Louisiana.

MY DAD
Sir Yellsalot

I think my dad actually would have made a pretty good knight. He likes to wax the car—so he'd probably keep his armor really shiny. And he collects garden gnomes—so I guess he'd get along with the magical elves and fairies of the medieval forest. I dunno about killing dragons, though. I mean, as it is, my dad likes wildlife an awful lot. (On the other hand, there's nobody more ferocious at slaying bugs!)

That is, until her seventh birthday came around. And the next sweet potato pie was baked, and the next "Happy Birthday" sung.

Being a year older, Darcy Lou was now a year wiser—and she no longer believed her father was a knight in King Arthur's court. So when *Tante* Dalphia again advised her to "Make a wish, make a wish, while the smoke's still here, and it'll take your wish to heaven, dear!" Darcy Lou made the exact same request—

Well, Darcy Lou, at least you're consistent, I'll say that for you.

"I wish I knew my daddy!"

This time, poor Tallulah's face went white as the petals of her terrestrial orchids.

"Your daddy," said elegant *Tante* Maribelle, as serious as ever. "Why, dear, don't you know? Your daddy was a . . . pirate."

Now, I cannot see my dad as a pirate. I mean . . . an earring? A head scarf? Yo-ho-hoing with a crew of riffraff? Nope. No way. On the other hand, there is his offspring—my scheming little brother, Matt, to be precise. Now, that boy is pirate material in the making. For sure.

"A pirate?" asked seven-year-old Darcy Lou.

"Oh, yes," said *Tante* Maribelle. "A first-rate pirate with his own pirate ship and crew. He sailed the West Indies, looking for gold and booty and—"

"Coca-Cola!" blurted jolly *Tante* Jo-Jo.

"And he wrestled alligators," added *Tante* Dalphia.

What the heck is pirate booty, anyway? I mean, besides a snack food. . .

Roosevelt, Franklin D., 32nd president of the United states from 1933 to 1945. Also Roosevelt, Theodore, 26th pres. of U.S., 1901–09.
(I looked it up.)

"And he took their skins to President Roosevelt, who threw him a *fais do-do,*" finished elegant *Tante* Maribelle with a face straighter than the buttons on her classic black-and-white-checked coatdress.

Fais do-do: What the Cajuns call an all-night dance with the old and the young invited. (Looked that up, too!)

And so, for her entire seventh year, Darcy Lou heard tales of her father the pirate. Until the next birthday, of course, when she'd outgrown pirate stories. That's when she found out her daddy was a cowboy, who broke broncs and shot a six-gun so well, they made him marshal of Dry Gulch, Arizona.

A cowboy? Yeah, I guess that's something my dad could've been. He likes animals, so he'd take care of the cows and horses pretty well. And, as far as marshaling, he's definitely got the whole "don't-break-my-rules-or-else!" thing down, too. . . .

In her ninth year, Darcy Lou's daddy was a painter, off studying in Italy with Michelangelo and Leonardo da Vinci. The year after that, he was a playwright working in England for some man named Shakespeare. And, after that, he was a novelist, helping Charles Dickens and H. G. Wells with their stories in London.

On her next birthday, which was her twelfth, Darcy Lou's father was an explorer who discovered the continent of Antarctica with Admiral Byrd.

At thirteen, he was a daring pilot who

Okay, so this girl Darcy's either playing along with the pretend thing, or she's the most gullible kid on earth, right? I mean Michelangelo and da Vinci and Shakespeare and Dickens and Wells had pretty much, like, exited the building for good by the time this book was even written!

helped the Wright brothers with their designs, taught Charles Lindbergh everything he knew, then disappeared into the mist with Amelia Earhart.

I wish my little brother, Matt, had disappeared into the mist with Amelia, too.

Which brought Darcy Lou to the day before her fourteenth birthday . . . and her *second* defining moment.

Another defining moment? Okay, I guess I'm sort of interested. . . .

Chapter 2

A Letter Home

"YOUR DADDY'S NOT A PILOT, Darcy Lou Beignet! You *never* had no daddy! I heard my mama say so!"

Those words of Adele Aleman's would haunt Darcy Lou for years to come. Mainly because they were shouted in front of the entire class at the newly opened public school, an hour's bus ride outside Bayou Le Blanc.

Until now, Darcy Lou had been schooled at home by her mother, who'd sent Darcy off without ever mentioning that attending *public* school meant *everything* about your life would be made *public*.

Tell me about it!

"You don't know nothin', Adele!" Darcy

In grade school I had a teacher with a funny name, too. Mr. Burr. Which doesn't sound funny by itself. But when the kids found out his first name was Tim, all you heard shouted in the halls was "Timber!"

Lou shouted right back. "My daddy was a great pilot. World famous. He flew with Charles Lindbergh and Amelia Earhart!"

"That's quite enough, Darcy Lou!" said their teacher, Mrs. Punaise, whose name had made Darcy Lou snicker from the outset, because in the Cajun French they used back home, *punaise* meant "stinkbug"—and how in the world could a person *not* laugh out loud when someone wrote, "My name is Mrs. Stinkbug" on the chalkboard?

It had all started the previous day, which was the first day of school, when Mrs. Punaise had assigned the class homework.

"Now I know many of you have been schooled at home up till now," she'd said. "So I want each of you to fill a notebook page with something about yourself and your family. Then I'll have each of you stand before the class and read your page. That way, I can see how well you read and write and express yourself. And we can all learn something about each of your families."

Glad I didn't have that assignment. I'd have to reveal my brother was left on our doorstep by aliens.

Darcy Lou could have written about how her mother grew orchids and played Cajun poker with her best friends on the big mahogany table every week. Or she could have written about how her grandpa was sickly and in bed most of the time. But she thought all that was plain boring. So instead, she wrote about all the fantastic stories her *tantes* had told her this past year about her daddy's adventures.

When her turn to speak had finally come, she shot right up, raced to the front of the schoolroom, and began to tell about the time her father had advised Orville and Wilbur Wright on how to make a plane out of a bicycle. That's when the teacher stopped her. And Adele Aleman, the most popular and meanest girl in the whole school, shouted those awful things about how Darcy had never had a father.

A story about aerodynamics? Sounds like the perfect girl for Tudgeman.

"Most popular and meanest." Now who does THAT sound like? Kate Sanders, Kate Sanders, Kate Sanders!

"Darcy Lou's a liar, Mrs. Punaise!" Adele shouted out.

"Yes," agreed the teacher in a cold, calm voice.

"It's not lying!" cried Darcy Lou. "It's just . . . just . . . "

"Just *what,*" said Mrs. Punaise, her mouth in a grim line, and the vein on her forehead thumping like a muskrat tail beneath a bayou mud bog.

Muskrat?
(Is that like a hamster? Or a rat that smells like musk?)

"Just *stories*," said Darcy Lou.

"Lies, girl, that's what you're telling," said Mrs. Punaise. "And I won't have lies in my classroom."

"Then what do you call those?" said Darcy Lou, pointing to a shelf of novels, almost all of which her mother had already made her read.

"And I certainly won't have insolence and rudeness! You are now to go to that chalkboard and write the truth a hundred times until you learn respect."

TOTAL HUMILIATION

Oh, wow, total humiliation in front of one's peers . . . been there, done that (still have the T-shirt!).

Darcy went to the chalkboard. She picked up the chalk. Then she stopped and turned around to face her teacher.

"Mrs. Punaise, what exactly do you want me to write?" she asked.

"I am a liar."

Darcy felt her face flushing hot. She felt tears sting her eyes, but she didn't want to cry. Not in front of everyone. Not in *public*.

I'll take "Reasons why I want to crawl into a bottomless hole" for one thousand, Alex!

All the kids were looking at her. Almost all of them were snickering. Then her eyes fell on a neighbor boy with sandy brown hair and a sprinkling of freckles. His name was

Gaston Guidry, but everybody knew him as Gator.

Darcy didn't know Gator very well—just enough to know he didn't like shoes and was partial to fishing poles, denim overalls, and chewing on long blades of onion weed he'd pluck from the banks of their bayou.

Gator's a cool nickname—sounds sort of like a bayou version of Gordo. . . .

But Gator was pretty nearly the only one *not* laughing at her. Instead, when he caught Darcy Lou's eye, he pointed at Mrs. Punaise and mouthed "Stinkbug." Then he put fingers on either end of his mouth, pulled his lips out like a clown, and stuck out his tongue.

This Gator guy's sort of acting like Gordo, too. (I mean, when we were younger. Gordo acts more mature now—usually.)

Mrs. Punaise was facing Darcy Lou, so she couldn't see Gator's joke. But Darcy did, and her tears turned into laughter.

"Something funny about what I've asked you to do, Darcy Lou?" asked Mrs. Punaise. "Because if there is, I'll have you see the principal. How would you like that?"

Now Gator was crossing his eyes.

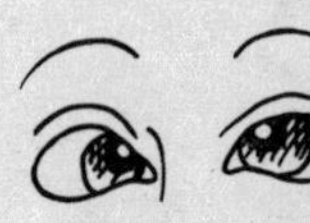

Darcy spun to face the chalkboard. She tried to write but couldn't. She was laughing too hard.

"Mr. Guidry!" cried the teacher, who by this time had turned around to find Gator making a fool of her. "Up! Out of that seat!"

Then Darcy Lou and Gator were both thrown out of class.

Ugh. I'm having an Angel Lieberman flashback.

"You shouldn't have got yourself into trouble," Darcy Lou told Gator in a prim voice as they sat in stiff wooden chairs beside a door marked PRINCIPAL'S OFFICE.

Double ugh. Now I'm having a Mr. Tweedy flashback!

"Aw, why not," said Gator. "Ol' Stinkbug's just a grouch. You shouldn't let her get to you like that."

"Like what?" Darcy Lou asked, nervously fiddling with the end of her long yellow braid.

"Whaddya mean, like what?" said Gator. "You looked about to cry."

"I was *not* about to cry," lied Darcy Lou.

"Were, too."

"Was not."

"Were, too."

"Was not!"

"Till I made you laugh," said Gator.

"Which is how we ended up here," said Darcy Lou. She noticed the principal's secretary staring at them over her big, black typewriter. Darcy gave the woman a weak smile, but the secretary just scowled and mumbled, "Troublemakers" under her breath.

Reminds me of my old dragon boss at the Digital Bean, constantly breathing down my neck, and muttering all sorts of unflattering things about me. And I only dropped all the silverware on the floor once—or twice. (Who knew a job would be so much . . . work!)

"That's what we'll be known as from now on, you know," whispered Gator as he elbowed Darcy gently in the ribs.

"What?" asked Darcy Lou.

"Troublemakers," he said. "Bad kids."

"Oh, no. Not me," said Darcy Lou. "My mama sent me here to be a good student, and that's what I aim to be."

"Ol' Stinkbug won't let you," said Gator, leaning back in his chair and putting a foot over his knee. "Mark my words, she'll have it in for both of us now."

"What do we do then?" asked Darcy Lou.

Gator shrugged. "Nothin' *to* do. Just gotta stick it out, I guess. Together."

Sounds like me and Gordo, all right. BFF in the making. (Best friends forever!)

Darcy Lou thought of all the kids snickering at her, and she felt the tears sting her eyes again.

"They all think they're better than me. But they're not," said Darcy Lou. "I'll show them, Gator. I will. Someday I'll show them all."

When Darcy Lou got off the school bus that afternoon, she didn't go home. She was too worried. The principal had scolded both Gator and Darcy Lou and given each of them a sealed letter addressed to their mothers.

The letter home. Yikes!

Darcy Lou was worried the letter would upset her mother, so she decided to show the letter to one of her aunts first and get some good advice.

Crazy *Tante* Dalphia lived in the city of New Orleans, so Darcy couldn't show her. And jolly *Tante* Jo-Jo wasn't at home. She'd gone into the city with a half dozen gowns she'd tailored for one of the shops on Canal Street. So she couldn't show her, either.

That left *Tante* Maribelle, who was the most elegant and well-spoken of all the aunts—but also the most serious and intimidating. That's why Darcy was reluctant to track her down.

In the past, Darcy would have had to

travel an hour by bus in order to visit Maribelle—because the woman had been a live-in nanny for some of the finest families in the city. But after Maribelle's father had passed away five years earlier, she'd inherited her old family home and moved back to Bayou Le Blanc.

Wow—everybody in our neighborhood just hires baby-sitters by the hour. Not an easy job to get, either. I still can't believe I had to stand on my head just to get my parents to let me baby-sit my stupid little brother. And it was about as pleasant as using your bare hands to dig up earthworms—AND I HATE EARTHWORMS!

Darcy Lou immediately recognized Maribelle's black Ford sedan on the dirt drive next to the house. As she approached the house's wide veranda, Darcy Lou noticed another car parked there. It was a little red sports car, a convertible with the roof down.

Darcy Lou had never seen a car like that around the bayou. Most of the vehicles around Darcy's home were mud-splattered old pick-ups. The red convertible looked awfully expensive. And Darcy Lou couldn't help admiring its sleek lines and gleaming surface, so shiny she could see her wide blue eyes reflecting back at her like she was looking into a polished red mirror.

When she heard voices coming from the house, she turned quickly and walked up

My mom told me Dad had this really old hatchback once that he hated to part with. But then things started falling off. Important things. Like the engine block.

the veranda steps. Obviously, someone had been visiting Maribelle, and he was about to come out the front door. Which brought Darcy Lou to the third defining moment of her life . . .

Whaddya know, another defining moment . . . Okay, I guess I'm still interested . . .

Chapter 3

Lightning Strike

"I SO ENJOYED TALKING WITH you again, Nanny," the young man said to Maribelle as he stepped toward the screen door.

He was like no other boy Darcy Lou had ever seen. Not in her entire fourteen years on earth. Tall and lean, he wore gray slacks with a knife-sharp crease, a snow-white shirt, and a beautiful blue jacket perfectly tailored to fit his lanky form. His jaw was square, his raven-black hair neatly cut and handsomely brushed back off his princely forehead.

I know THAT feeling . . . (sigh) Lizzie ❤ Ethan

When he turned toward her, Darcy Lou

He sounds DEELISH!

saw that he was older than she was, but not by much. Perhaps sixteen or so. Certainly in high school.

Darcy Lou had been so entranced, she just stood there, still as a statue as he swung the screen door open.

Oh, wow. Locker door flashback! Glad to know I'm not the only one who has close encounters with hinged things!

BAM! Right in Darcy Lou's forehead.

The sharp knock didn't hurt Darcy Lou, but it startled her, and she stumbled back on the veranda. She then lost her balance and fell right down the front steps, landing on the walkway, flat on her back.

"Oh, no!" exclaimed the young man as he rushed forward, Maribelle right on his heels.

"Little girl, are you all right?" he asked, bending over her.

"Little girl?" What's he talking about? She's fourteen! (Unless, of course, she's wearing a dorky outfit that makes her look like a little girl. Like when my parents once made me wear that heinous unicorn sweater that made me look eight—and I was thirteen at the time. Too awful.

Darcy Lou was mortified, her face as red as a steamed crawfish shell. She sat up and looked through her golden bangs into eyes greener than swamp gas.

Then she sighed. She wanted to answer, but no words seemed to be forthcoming. None that made any sense, that is.

"I think she's in shock," the young man said with a tone of great concern.

This whole thing reminds me of when I had to practice keeping my tongue untied before asking Ethan to the Sadie Hawkins dance. I used Gordo as the stand-in for Ethan. (I don't think Gordo liked it much.)

The McGuire coat of arms

Tante Maribelle bent down and studied Darcy's flushed face and awestruck gaze.

"Yes, I think she is," said Maribelle. "But not the kind you mean, William. I think she's just shocked to find a boy like you in Bayou Le Blanc. Am I right, Darcy Lou, honey?"

My coat of arms

Darcy Lou nodded and noticed a crest on the pocket of William's shirt. It looked like a coat of arms, the kind princes and knights had in the books she'd read.

"This was entirely my fault, miss," drawled the young man named William. "Please accept my profound apologies."

Uh-hem! From my unique historical perspective as a 21st-century teen, I have a hard time believing any boy ever spoke like that! Note to Mr. Dig: how did boys talk when you were fourteen?

Darcy was stunned by William's politeness. No bayou boy had ever spoken to her like that! She wished she could think of something just as wonderful to say. Something brilliant, and witty, and genteel.

"May I assist you to your feet?" he asked, offering his hand.

"Um . . . sure," said Darcy Lou. "Um . . . thanks."

She placed her small palm against his larger one, and the young man gave Darcy

Way to go, Darcy. That's exactly the kind of sparkling wit I use whenever Ethan's around!

Lou a smile as dazzling as the white-hot rays of the southern summer sun. And that's when she felt it . . . the lightning bolt.

It struck her with the swiftness of a thunder clap, the power of a gulf-storm hurricane. It shook her with the force of a dozen possibilities, a hundred "what ifs?," a thousand divine daydreams, a million marvelous maybes. It electrified her mind, awakened her senses, magnetized her hair. . . .

Crush-boy victim

Wow, is she blissed out or what?!

Instantly, Darcy knew she would be thinking about William in every lazy moment, dreaming of him every night after she fell asleep.

She pictured him in a handsome tuxedo, dancing with her around a glittering ballroom; envisioned him standing at the end of a long aisle, beneath a bower of flowers, ready to say "I, William, take you, Darcy Lou Beignet . . ."

When she got to her feet, the young man bent down again. "Did you drop this?" he asked.

The letter from the principal! thought Darcy. Oh, no!

Darcy Lou snatched it out of his hand and hid it behind her back.

William's raised eyebrows made her wince. All of a sudden, she realized how rude she'd just acted, grabbing the letter like that right out of his hand.

"I'm sorry," she managed to choke out, mentally kicking herself. "And, um . . . thank you . . . again."

Then Darcy Lou's wide blue eyes just stared.

The young man nodded and turned to Maribelle. "Well, I really must be going now, Nanny. You know, you are so very sweet to let me keep calling you Nanny."

"Oh, it's just between us, William," said Maribelle. "Now you run along and be a good boy."

William laughed as he went to his little red sports car. "That's what you used to tell me when I was nine," he told Maribelle.

"It's still good advice," she told him.

"Happy birthday again, Nanny!" he called, starting up the engine.

When the little red sports car was nothing

HOW EMBARRASSING

more than a cloud of dust down the road, Darcy Lou turned to her aunt and asked in a spellbound voice, "Who was that boy?"

"William Chatelaine of the Garden District Chatelaines," said Maribelle. "William's uncle is a former state governor, his father a respected judge. I was their family nanny for eight years. William was five when I started."

"How old is he now?" asked Darcy Lou.

"Sixteen. But I left them when he was thirteen," said Maribelle. "Did you see that crest on his blazer pocket?"

Darcy nodded.

"That's St. Thomas Boys' Preparatory Academy, the best precollege curriculum in New Orleans. His family has high expectations for him, I can tell you. He wants more than anything to live up to them."

I wonder what "expectations" my parents have for me. Actually, I'm pretty sure they'll be happy if I manage to graduate without any strange piercings or visible tattoos!

"And he came to wish you a happy birthday?" asked Darcy Lou. "But your birthday was last week."

"Indeed. He said he wanted to come last week, but he only just received the car today. And he also confessed he'd always wanted to see Bayou Le Blanc. Now that he has his own transportation, he found his way down here."

"How did he know about our bayou?" asked Darcy.

"Oh, well, I'd told him and his younger sister many a Cajun folk tale when they were growing up, so naturally he was always curious."

Danger! Do Not Open. May cause Stomach Upset!

"Do tell."

"Yes, and DO tell me what's in that letter you so rudely grabbed from Master William," said Maribelle. "The one you're still hiding behind your back."

"It's . . . complicated—"

"Give it here, child," demanded Maribelle.

Darcy held it out for her aunt, who read the envelope and said, "Why, this letter is for your mother. And it's from your principal! What's the meaning of this, Darcy Lou?"

Tweedy alert! Principals are like doctors. You only see them when something goes majorly wrong. And then there's always some prescription to remedy the problem that's, like, really hard to swallow.

"I wanted you to read it before Mama, because . . . well," said Darcy Lou, "she might get upset, and I thought you could help."

"If you've done something wrong, Darcy Lou, you can't expect me to stop your mother from disciplining you. You should know that."

Darcy's such a saint. I, personally, would be sweating the parental sentencing about now. . .

Grounded . . . until eligible for Social Security

"Oh, I'm not worried about being disciplined," said Darcy Lou. "I don't care about that. I'm worried about Mama. I know what sorts of things make her feel bad. And this is one of them. I'm just worried about her feelings."

"Well, I can't open a letter that's addressed to someone else. That's not proper," said Maribelle.

"But—"

"*But,*" interrupted Maribelle, "you can *tell* me what this is all about."

And Darcy Lou did.

An hour later, Maribelle was speaking quietly with Darcy Lou's mother, Tallulah, at the big mahogany table in the Beignet dining room.

Darcy waited on the porch swing, listening to the sounds around her—the cricket chirps and birdcalls, the splash of a frog in the nearby slow-moving water, the high-pitched bleating *kee-er!* of a royal tern.

Around the house, a slight breeze stirred

the Spanish moss in the oak and cypress trees, and the sweet smell of her mother's orchid garden made Darcy Lou sigh with appreciation for her bayou home.

Finally, she heard the creak and rattle of the old screen door. *Tante* Maribelle stood on the veranda, holding it open.

"Your mother is waiting for you, Darcy Lou," she said. "Go on in."

Ugh. The moment of truth.

As Maribelle departed, Darcy Lou stepped into the cool shade of the big house.

Tallulah was coming out of the kitchen, wiping her eyes. In her hand, she held the open letter from the principal.

Why are principals such grinches? Like when Principal Tweedy banned me from the Spring Fling dance because I took the blame when Kate broke the statue of the school's first principal— whose most memorable words were "Cut that out!" Now if that doesn't prove my point about principals, I don't know what does!!

"Oh, Mama, don't cry!" Darcy Lou ran to Tallulah, throwing her arms around the waist of her mother's faded cotton dress.

"It's all right, honey," said Tallulah.

"It's all my fault!" Darcy Lou wailed. "Please don't be upset with me—"

"Oh, sweet potato," said Tallulah, "I'm not upset with you. I'm upset with myself. It's all *my* fault. Not yours. Come with me."

Tallulah lead Darcy upstairs, to Tallulah's bedroom, a cheerful place with yellow curtains

Job: principal
Skills needed . . .
* Good lungs (for yelling at kids all day)
* Enjoy sending poison pen letters home to parents.
* Be total grouch.

and flowered wallpaper. Darcy sat on the homemade yellow-and-blue quilt that covered the big bed.

"It's long past time we straightened out that business about your father," said Tallulah as she reached under the bed. "The Orchids and Gumbo Poker Club thought you were too young to understand the truth. And they like to spin yarns. But I should have put a stop to their yarns about your daddy. I was wrong to encourage the stories. It just confused you, and now look what's happened."

"You weren't wrong," said Darcy Lou. "I *knew* they were just stories. I've known that for years! There's nothing wrong with stories. Stories are a lot more interesting than real life . . . and, I expect, a lot more cheerful, too. And I didn't want to see you unhappy, so I went along."

"You did," said Tallulah. "And I told myself it was all right because you were young. But you're older now. My! Time passes so quickly! I guess, I'll always see you as my little girl, but the truth is you're becoming a young woman. Even though I'd like to keep you little forever,

". . . becoming a young woman. . . ." SHUDDER! How I hate that phrase. Reminds me of when my mom came with Miranda and me to the women's undergarment department at the mall and we tried to buy me my first . . . oh, forget it. It's just way too embarrassing!

keep you safe and close, here with me, I know it's time I recognized that you're growing up, growing older." Tallulah placed a hatbox on the bed. "You're old enough now to hear the truth about your daddy. Am I right, sweet potato?"

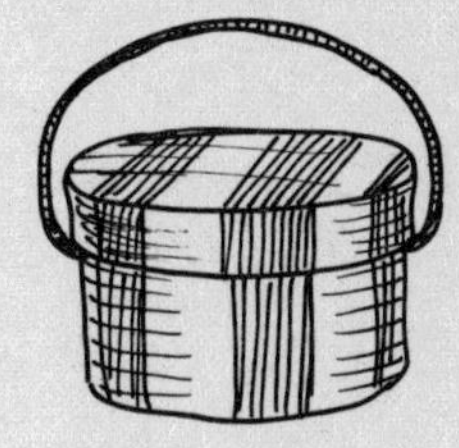

What truth? Daddy liked to wear women's hats?!

Darcy Lou nodded.

"Funny, you know, your daddy used to call me that, too. . . . "

"Sweet potato?"

"Sweet potato" is such an adorable nickname! Around my house, the closest thing I have to a nickname is "Hey, clean-your-room."

"Yes, because I so loved sweet potato pie . . . still do." Tallulah opened the big hatbox and sat down next to it. "Your father's name was Ben Terpen, and he wanted more than anything to be a writer. I still have a few of his stories if you'd like to read them."

Tallulah showed Darcy Lou a bundle of neatly typewritten pages, tied together with string. Darcy Lou's eyes widened as she took them into her hands. She read the titles of the stories aloud and the words beneath them, "By Ben Terpen."

One story was a western, about a cowboy who became a marshal. And another was a story about a pilot. It was even illustrated

USS *Darcy's Dad*—
GO Navy!

with little paintings on small cards, which Tallulah said were done by Darcy Lou's father, too.

"Ben was drafted into the navy before he could go to college," continued Tallulah. "He was stationed near here, and we met in New Orleans."

Tallulah showed Darcy Lou a picture of her father, a tall, handsome man with dark hair in a navy uniform. He stood with his arm around a much younger Tallulah, who was displaying the happiest smile Darcy had ever seen her mother wear.

"We fell in love, and he proposed marriage," said Tallulah, opening a small square box. "He gave me this bracelet because he couldn't afford a ring."

Yellowing photo from a hatbox: $2; economical bracelet of engagement: $20; truth about your dad: priceless. . . .

Darcy fingered the pretty bracelet, amazed that her very own father had picked it out, had held it, had given it with the promise of everlasting love.

"He said he'd buy me a proper wedding ring when we got married, but they shipped him out so suddenly, with no notice, that we didn't have time. I discovered I was expecting you the same day I got the news that he had been killed in action."

"So . . ." said Darcy Lou, after thinking about it, "in a way my daddy was sort of a knight, after all, and a pirate, and a writer, and a painter—"

"And a pilot," said Tallulah. "He'd learned how to fly planes because he'd worked as a crop duster in Texas. But, I'm sorry to say, your <u>daddy was an orphan</u> and had no other family. So there was no one on his side to tell about your being born."

Woe—
tragedy city

"My daddy was a lot of wonderful things, wasn't he?" said Darcy Lou.

"Yes, he was, sweet potato. The Orchids and Gumbo Poker Club are my best friends in the whole world. They knew your father. And they knew how much I loved him. They just wanted to protect you and me from pain . . . so they turned it all into a game—<u>embroidered the truth</u>. . . . "

"Embroidered the truth," huh? Good one. I'll have to remember that little phrase next time I meet a girl like Angel Lieberman and I have to come up with some explanation for getting detention and wearing a temporary nose ring.

"Embroidered," said Darcy Lou. "Yes, I see. But Mrs. Punaise and the principal—they say it's a lie. And they called me a liar."

"No, sweet potato, you're not a liar. What

the Orchids and Gumbo Poker Club did was never meant to cause any harm. But now it's harmed you, and we need to set things right."

"Oh, I don't care about me," said Darcy Lou. "I just care about you. I don't want to see you sad. Not ever."

"Oh, sweet potato, you are the best daughter a mother could ever have." Tallulah hugged Darcy Lou close. "I'm sorry about what happened at school, but I'll have a talk with your principal to explain it all. And someday, I promise, I'll make this up to you. I want us to be friends. Friends forever."

"We will be, Mama. I promise," said Darcy Lou. "I love you, and that's all that matters to me."

"Me, too, sweet potato. Me, too."

I have to admit, I feel the same way about my mom. I don't like seeing her sad, either. . . . (For one thing, it has a really heinous effect on the edibility of her cooking . . . and indigestion is never a good idea.)

I wonder if my mom thinks of me as her friend? We never talk like this. I mean, my father's no big mystery or anything, so there's no need for the Hatbox Talk. But I bet there are lots of things on her mind she could totally talk over with me. Stuff that could be just between us. That'd be really cool. . . . I wonder how she'd feel about calling me "sweet potato"?

Chapter 4
Alligator Chicken

THE YEAR FLEW BY LIKE A PASSING flock of hungry white egrets, and every week, like gossipy clockwork, the Orchids and Gumbo Poker Club met at Tallulah's house to play cards.

The women never asked Darcy Lou to join them at the big mahogany table in the dining room, which was regularly set with a vase of Tallulah's delicate orchids and a pot of *Tante* Jo-Jo's delicious seafood gumbo. They considered Darcy too young to join their talks. But Darcy would always hang around nearby, in the kitchen, to eavesdrop.

"How's school, Darcy Lou?" one of her aunts would always ask when she'd come around the table to pour out a pitcher of mint iced tea.

"Okay," she would always say.

But it wasn't okay.

Don't feel bad, Darcy Lou—at least you didn't enter a Spanish language game show and not even know how to speak Spanish . . . not one of my better ideas.

The Orchids and Gumbo Poker Club might have understood and accepted the idea of "embroidering" the truth, but Darcy Lou's schoolteacher did not.

"Benjamin Franklin was *not* the first man to journey to the planet Mars, Darcy Lou Beignet!" cried Mrs. Punaise one day.

"But he might have—and not mentioned it to anyone," she told her teacher. "Doesn't it make the report more interesting?"

"It does not. And it forces me to grade your paper—which is *otherwise* excellent in grammar, spelling, and historical detail—as a D."

Oh, way harsh curve!

Socially, Darcy had her challenges, too. That original report she'd made in front of the class, about her pilot daddy knowing the Wright brothers, Charles Lindbergh, and Amelia Earhart, had haunted her for the entire school year. Just when she thought her class-

"Socially" challenged? Yeah, that's how I feel half the time!

Hmmmm . . .
I wonder if I could get school funding for an official "socially challenged" after-school, group? . . .
Nah. Scratch that. Bad idea. Like REALLY nuclear bad!

mates had stopped snickering about it, Adele Aleman would remind them.

"Hey, look," Adele shouted in the lunchroom one day when Darcy Lou had trouble finding an empty seat. "It's that Beignet girl."

Standing in the middle of the room, holding her metal lunch tray, Darcy Lou could feel her face blushing a hundred shades of red.

"Didn't you disappear with Amelia?" shouted Adele. "Oh, no, that was your vanishing daddy, wasn't it?"

Ugh. What a Kate Sanders moment. Obviously, this Adele Aleman person has the 1950s version of cheerleader superpowers.

Darcy Lou hated confrontations. She just kept her head down and hoped nobody would pay attention. But everybody was paying attention. In fact, everybody was staring at Darcy Lou, waiting to see what she would do next.

Can somebody tell me, please, what went wrong with human evolution? I mean, what other so-called intelligent life-form has turned humiliation of its own kind into a spectator sport?!

"There's a seat, over here," a familiar voice suddenly said.

Gaston "Gator" Guidry had stood up at his table and waved her over. He was easy to see, because he was quickly growing into one of the tallest and strongest boys in her class. Darcy Lou breathed a sigh of relief as she headed his way. Thank goodness that's over, she thought to herself—until she heard Gator shout across the room, "Hey, Adele, do you know that you're famous?"

"No," said Adele, batting her long dark eyelashes as if Gator were flirting with her.

A lot of boys had crushes on Adele, so why not Gator, too? After all, Adele was attractive enough. She had long curly brown hair, perfect skin, and she was constantly wearing brand-new, beautifully coordinated outfits. Her family owned a number of clothing stores, so she was always decked out like a Sears catalog model—in everything from slim-line pencil skirts and matching sweaters to pretty polka-dot dresses with flouncy petticoats underneath.

Whaddya know . . . a fashionista circa 1950! (I didn't think they even existed way back in the olden days.)

"What makes you think I'm famous, Gator?" called Adele, coyly. "Did you see a model in some magazine advertisement that looked like me?"

"Oh, no. Nothing like that," Gator shouted back. "My uncle said he just bought the most ornery, foul-smelling mule in the bayou, and he needed a name. So, of course, I told him to name her Adele."

Ha! Ha-ha-ha-ha!

I wonder what Kate would do if Gordo shouted something like that at her!

For a moment, the entire lunchroom was dead silent. Then, like a sudden tidal wave, a roar of laughter rose up and broke over the room. Adele Aleman was stunned into silence, her face turning beet red with humiliation and fury.

"Why'd you do that?" Darcy Lou snapped at Gator after sitting down next to him.

The place had gone crazy with hoots and laughter and shouts of "hee-haw!" The commotion was so bad, a teacher had to race into the lunchroom to quiet everyone down.

"Whaddya mean, *why* did I do that?" said Gator. "I did it to stick up for you . . . to help."

Gator is such a cool friend. He really does remind me of Gordo. . . .

"But it's not going to help," said Darcy Lou. "Adele will just be angrier than ever now."

"So what?" said Gator. "Sometimes you just have to stand up for yourself, no matter what the consequences."

"Oh, it's so easy?" said Darcy Lou.

"It is," said Gator. "I mean, if Adele was making fun of me, I probably would have let it go. But she wasn't making fun of me. She was making fun of my friend. And when you see a friend is being treated bad . . . I don't know, Darcy Lou . . . I can't explain it."

"I don't understand you, Gator."

"Aw, just forget it," said Gator. "Maybe someday you will."

Well, I understand him! That's why I jumped in front of Miranda when she was getting splashed with green paint because some witchy fashionista who was wearing the same outfit wanted to ruin it before school pictures were taken!

Gator did turn out to be a good friend to Darcy Lou. During summer recess, he started stopping by the house when he saw Darcy out on the veranda swing.

Once a week, he'd even take her fishing in his pirogue. And when they caught something good, Tallulah would fry it up for dinner.

Fishing. Right. That would involve worms. And I never, ever want to see, touch, or smell another earthworm. Not after that science camping trip when I had to help repopulate the class worm farm. Yuck.

Then school started again, and, except for Darcy Lou's being fifteen instead of fourteen, everything went back to the way it had been. Adele was still just as popular and just as stuck-up, and her teacher—a man named Mr. Hamburg—still had no appreciation for "embroidered" reports.

The one thing that stood out in Darcy Lou's memory as anything remotely close to a defining moment that year was her second meeting with William Chatelaine.

A "pirogue" is not, in fact, a Polish dumpling, which is what I thought it was when I first read this. (The dumpling thing is a pierogi, not a pirogue! And how could you go fishing in a Polish dumpling, anyway?!)

Uh-hem . . . "pirogues" are what the Cajuns call their small, narrow rowboats—sort of like canoes.

He'd come by in the early fall, just as he had the year before, to wish his former nanny a happy birthday. On her way home from the bus stop, Darcy Lou recognized the little red sports car immediately. It was parked, as it had been the year before, right beside Maribelle's big old Ford. Darcy Lou couldn't help but stop and admire William's convertible for a long time—as long as it took William to finally come out and notice her, that is!

"Good afternoon, miss," William Chatelaine said, when he finally approached his car.

Darcy Lou nervously toed the dirt with her scuffed-up shoe. Raven-haired William Chatelaine had grown even handsomer over the past year, if that was possible. He wore the same gray slacks and blue blazer with the St. Thomas Boys' Preparatory Academy crest. But his shoulders seemed broader, his height a little taller, his eyes even *greener* than swamp gas.

Excuse me, but what the heck is swamp gas? And, more important, what the heck does it smell like?! EWWW!

Suddenly, Darcy Lou wished she could snap her fingers and become a completely different person. Oh, how she wanted to exchange her little-girl cotton jumper for what

Hello! She wants to snap her fingers and be totally different? Welcome to my world!

Adele Aleman had been wearing that day: a classy-looking-houndstooth-check slim skirt, matching gold sweater, and high-heeled pumps.

But Darcy Lou couldn't snap her fingers and change. So instead, she tried to collect herself quickly. Then she cleared her throat and said as properly as she could manage, "Good afternoon, Mr. Chatelaine."

William Chatelaine looked caught by surprise. "Do I know you, miss? You seem to know *me*. Have we met?"

"Last year," said Darcy Lou. "I, uh, had a little accident with the screen door up there on the veranda."

"A little accident"? The guy beaned her so hard she fell into next week!

"Oh, yes, of course!" exclaimed William, then he laughed. "But I don't believe we were properly introduced."

Of course, they weren't "properly introduced"! Darcy was too busy trying to figure out whether she was suffering from a concussion or a really bad crush. The symptoms, it seems to me, are an awful lot alike (frightening isn't it?!).

"No," said Darcy. "You see, after you drove away last year, I asked *Tante* Maribelle your name." Then Darcy cleared her throat again, offered her hand to shake, and said, "I'm Darcy Lou Beignet."

"Enchanted, Miss Beignet," said William. He bent over her hand and kissed it. "Are you

I never had a guy kiss my hand. I wonder what you're supposed to do. Just stand there, I guess. But what if he slobbers all over it? Are you allowed to wipe it off on your jeans, or is that like a dorkarella move?

as sweet as the beignet pastries I've sampled at Café du Monde?"

So I looked up "beignet"—it's not just Darcy's last name. Apparently it's also a pastry made of fried dough, which is then sprinkled with tons of powdered sugar. In New Orleans, they're served as a dessert or snack with coffee. Yum!

Darcy Lou nearly swooned. For a moment, she was speechless. Then, finally, she managed to ask, "How was your visit today?"

"Very pleasant, thank you, Miss Beignet," William drawled, leaning one hand against his red convertible. "Of course, I've always wanted to see more of the bayou. I take it you've lived here all your life?"

"Yes, Mr. Chatelaine. Of course, in my *imagined* life I've been to many other places."

"Your *imagined* life?"

My imagined life isn't nearly so elaborate. I just want Ethan Craft to ask me to ONE school dance.

"Oh, yes. I've been to Paris to see the Eiffel Tower, I've been to London to see Shakespeare performed by the Royal Company, to China to see the Great Wall . . . and I've been to outer space, too . . . to the moon and the stars . . . like Peter Pan flying into the night. . . . "

William Chatelaine stared, openmouthed, at Darcy Lou. He looked so shocked, she couldn't help laughing out loud.

"We like to spin yarns 'round here," she explained. "It makes life ever so much more interesting. It's the Cajun way."

"How adorable you are," said William, and he gave her the most charming smile. "Well, you know, I'd love to hear more about the bayou. When Miss Maribelle was our nanny, she told us many tales, and my own life's become a bit of a bore, to be honest—just a dreadful round of studying, stuffy garden parties, and my father's insisting I learn the game of golf. A vicious game. Beastly, if you ask me."

Golf, huh? Ethan actually likes golf. Well . . . nobody's perfect. And it could be worse. He could like River Dancing.

"You think *golf* is a beastly game?" said Darcy Lou. "I wonder what you'd think of one of our bayou games. I think you'd change your tune about golf, pretty darned fast."

"Oh, is that so? Do you have a game in mind, then?"

Darcy Lou shrugged. "How about Alligator Chicken?"

"Alligator Chicken?" said William Chatelaine. "What, pray tell, is that?"

"Shall I show you? Or are *you* a chicken?"

William Chatelaine's eyebrows rose. "A challenge, eh?"

Darcy Lou laughed.

"All right, Miss Beignet. You've more than sparked my curiosity. You're on!"

I hope Darcy's not going to feed a chicken to an alligator or something gross like that. I'll totally never forgive Mr. Dig if that's what comes next in this book!

"You'll have to come into the swamp," warned Darcy Lou. "Better leave your blazer here."

William Chatelaine nodded and carefully removed his blue blazer; then he neatly rolled up the sleeves of his white shirt. "What next?"

Darcy Lou piled her schoolbooks on the hood of William Chatelaine's car, kicked off her shoes, and pulled off her white ankle socks. Then she pointed to his feet.

"Better take off your shoes and socks, too. And roll up your pant legs."

William looked skeptical, but he did what she advised. "Lead on," he finally told her.

Darcy did. In her bare feet, she took him down a dirt path beside Maribelle's old house. When they reached the bank of the bayou, she walked along it, William's own bare feet treading right behind her. For ten minutes, they walked in silence, tearing through vines and stepping around the giant knobby roots of ancient cypress trees.

"What's that bird?" he suddenly asked,

pointing to a long-beaked beauty with a seven-foot-wide wingspan.

"A brown pelican," said Darcy Lou. "See how it's flying over the river?"

"Yes. Why is it doing that?"

"It's looking for some dinner."

"Dinner?"

"My, you really are a city boy," said Darcy Lou. "Just watch."

Sure enough, within the next few minutes, the big bird plunged dramatically, dropping from the sky like a dive bomber. Opening its long beak, it skimmed the water amid a school of fish, scooping up several before rising again.

Darcy pointed out the struggling tail fin hanging from the beak. The fin disappeared into the newly bulging pouch of the brown pelican's throat. Then the bird flapped its massive wings and rose high into the sky again.

"That was amazing," said William. "Marvelous."

"You *do* know the brown pelican's the Louisiana state bird, don't you?"

"It is?" said William. "I didn't know."

"Why, William Chatelaine," said Darcy Lou in a teasing voice, "I'm surprised at you. The nephew to a former governor, and you don't even know the state bird!"

William laughed, then quietly recited, as if to himself: "'He prayeth well who loveth well, both man and bird and beast. . . .'"

Overhearing, Darcy Lou couldn't help adding, "'He prayeth best, who loveth best, all things both great and small: for the dear God who loveth us, he made and loveth all.'"

Quoting poetry is so totally romantic! I wish I could quote poetry with Ethan, but I doubt he even knows any poetry. ("Ring Around the Rosy" doesn't count.)

William stopped and stared at Darcy Lou. "*You* know 'The Rime of the Ancient Mariner'?"

"Of course," said Darcy Lou. "Samuel Coleridge. Do you think I'm an illiterate hick just because I take off my shoes to walk in the swamps? I'll have you know my daddy was a writer, and he left my mama a house full of books."

"I see," said William. "And how did you know my uncle was once the governor?"

"Maribelle told me."

"Oh, yes. Of course."

No secrets in the bayou, eh? I can see the bayou has an awful lot in common with the Hillridge Junior High girls' lavatory!

"No secrets in the bayou, William."

"I can see that, Darcy Lou. It's more survival of the fittest, here, isn't it?"

"Yes," said Darcy Lou. "I'm sure Darwin would agree." She gave him a sly smile. "Are you ready to see how fit you are?"

Charles Darwin: naturalist who put forward the idea of "natural selection" as a theory of evolution. (I actually didn't have to look that up. Thank goodness, something from science class actually stuck with me!)

"I don't know about Darwin, but I never did claim I was Tarzan," William quipped with a wink. "But I'm willing to venture farther into your little jungle. So lead on, Jane."

When the slow-moving river veered off into a brackish branch, Darcy Lou motioned for him to follow quietly.

Birdcalls sounded all around them, and the earth became softer and wetter, the farther they moved into the thickening vegetation. The Spanish moss hung low from tree branches, blocking much of the sun, and the warm air was cloying with the fragrance of flowers and damp greenery. Soon their feet, and then their ankles, were sinking under the swampy mud with every step.

Gordo on evolution: "Humans are not the end result of predictable evolutionary progress. We're more like an accidental twig on a branch hanging on the edge of the universe."

"Darcy Lou, are you sure there are alligators back here?" asked William. The farther they moved into the swamp, the darker and

Me on evolution: "A primary example of evidence of the existence of the evolutionary ladder (particularly life-forms as ranked from lowest to highest) is the lunchroom at Hillridge Junior High!"

danker their surroundings became. The deep bayou was a spooky place to newcomers, and the tension in William's voice betrayed his understandable uneasiness.

"There are five hundred thousand alligators in the state of Louisiana," Darcy told him, matter-of-factly. "And Gator and I must have met at least half of them back here."

"Who is Gator?" asked William.

"Gaston Guidry. Just a friend. Now keep quiet and keep walking."

After a few more minutes, Darcy Lou told William to hold up. "There," she said, pointing. "A pair of gators."

"Where?" asked William, trying to shoo away a cloud of insects.

Darcy Lou pointed to what looked like two gray-green logs floating among reeds in the shallow water.

"They're treading water," she whispered.

"I can hardly see them," William whispered back.

"Time to play Alligator Chicken," she told him.

"And how are we to do that?"

Oh, no. PLEASE, don't let this be some sort of weird voodoo ritual where you feed live poultry to giant reptiles!

Come on in, the water's fine! (Tee-hee-hee!)

"You have to get down low." Darcy walked over to a three-hundred-year-old cypress and climbed onto one of its huge roots, which stuck out of the water like a giant's leg. She pressed her body down low against it.

William followed her example and crouched on another root right next to her. As he did, Darcy tried not to think about how wonderful the warmth of his bare forearm felt brushing against her shoulder.

That's how I felt when Ethan was knocked into me in the cafeteria line on the day of the chocolate brownie riots (sigh).

"What now?" asked William.

Darcy felt her heart beating fast, her palms sweating, her mouth drying up. Being this close to William was certainly affecting her in strange ways. Trying to keep her voice steady, she whispered, "We wait."

Remember, a pirogue is not a big potato dumpling.

On Gator's pirogue, Darcy Lou had seen alligators move through the water like silent gray ghosts. If she didn't keep an eye on them, they would sneak up on her without the slightest sound. And then she wouldn't be Darcy Lou Beignet anymore. She'd be lunch.

So Darcy kept her eyes glued to the two gators. She judged one of them to be about eight feet long, and the other twelve.

"That big one's four hundred pounds, easy," whispered Darcy Lou.

The gators were treading water with their heads and backs almost fully exposed on the surface. In the next moment, both completely submerged themselves, vanishing without making the slightest ripple.

"Where did they go?" asked William, his voice more than a little anxious.

"Keep watching the water," said Darcy Lou. "This is the *chicken* part of Alligator Chicken."

Oh! I get it. They're playing "chicken"—like who's going to blink first, the alligator or the human. Yikes!. Given a choice, I'd rather dig up earthworms—and we know how I feel about earthworms!

"What do you mean?"

"I mean, as long as we're crouched low like this, the alligators will think we're easy prey."

"You mean they're *hunting* us?"

"Of course," said Darcy Lou.

"Oh, my goodness."

"Well, William, you said you wanted to see more of the bayou, didn't you?"

Suddenly, the logs emerged from the brackish water again. They were only about twenty feet away now, and they numbered *more* than two. Darcy Lou counted eight alligators in all, treading water slowly toward them.

"You ready to call chicken?" asked Darcy Lou.

I'm with Willy!

"Oh, my goodness, yes," said William. "What do we do?"

"We just stand up," said Darcy Lou. "Watch." She stood up abruptly, and the alligators immediately eased off. "They don't like prey as tall as we are. Not that they couldn't tear us to pieces if they caught hold of us—"

"I think it's time to leave," said William.

"If you say so," said Darcy Lou.

She led him out of the dank swamp and back to the slow-moving river. When they reached the sunny, open area along the bank, William let out a huge sigh.

"Are you all right?" asked Darcy Lou.

"That was . . . thrilling!" cried William, picking Darcy Lou up and twirling her around. "Truly exciting!"

Darcy Lou laughed. How she loved the feeling of being hugged by William. She could feel her heart racing, her breath quickening, her face reddening.

Funny, how hugging a guy you like has the same effect as running a mile in gym class.

"That was nothing," said Darcy Lou when William put her down again. "My friend Gator lets them get plenty closer than that."

"You're joking," said William.

"He hunts them for meat for his family," she said, "so he has to."

"You mean he kills them?" asked William. "By hand?"

"Well, not by *bare* hand," said Darcy Lou. "He uses an alligator hook."

"No hunting rifle?" asked William.

"No. Just a hook," said Darcy Lou. "You can do it easy if you know what you're doing. Gator goes really deep into these swamps, too. A lot deeper than I've ever gone."

"Fascinating," said William. "But doesn't he get lost?"

"Never. He uses the trees and plants to guide his way. That boy can tell the difference between a bald cypress and a pond cypress at fifty paces. Folks around here say they've never seen anybody as good as Gator."

When they neared Maribelle's house, Darcy Lou showed William how to wash off

I wonder what my mom would make with alligator meat. Alligator stroganoff? Yuck. Don't even go there. . . .

I think Gordo would hunt alligators if he had to do it to feed his family. But he'd probably figure out a way to outsmart them—like luring them over a ditch covered with some elaborate vines or something. Gordo's just not an alligator hook type of guy!

his muddy feet in the river, then walk through the soft moss and grass to keep them clean. Finally, they reached the drive where his car sat, and both of them pulled on their socks and shoes.

"Thank you, Miss Beignet," said William before he climbed back into his car and drove away. "That was a marvelous experience for me!"

I totally know how Darcy feels! Ethan gave me a little excited half-hug once when I told him about a big sale on golf shoes at the mall, and I refused to wash my shirt for a week ('cause it smelled like his cologne . . . sigh).

"For me, too," said Darcy Lou, although she well knew *her* reasons for finding it a marvelous experience probably had nothing to do with his.

For months, Darcy dreamed of William Chatelaine. Over and over, she replayed his kissing her hand, laughing at her jokes, calling her adorable, brushing against her shoulder by that old cypress tree, and finally picking her up in his arms and twirling her around!

Normally, she would have confided in her mother what she was feeling. She told Tallulah everything, always. But, for the first time, Darcy kept her thoughts to herself.

Confided everything to her mother? Always? Hmmm . . .

I do like talking to my mom, when we actually talk. What I can't stand is when she just gives me the standard U.M.F. lines. (United Mom Front—the organization that trains moms to give simplistic answers to life's most difficult problems. Like—"Oh, honey, it's just hormones." Or: "Tomorrow is another day." Or: "Smile and the world smiles with you!") Grrrrrr . . . !

It wasn't that she didn't want her mother to know. Darcy simply felt that if she actually *talked* about her feelings for William, some wonderful spell would be broken. So, for a long time, she kept her secret feelings all to herself.

Darcy Lou also kept to herself the fact that what she wanted most was to see William again. But she didn't have a clue how to make it happen.

Eventually, however, an opportunity presented itself. Her mother began to take on more flower shop clients for her orchid corsages. This meant Tallulah now had to make weekly deliveries throughout the city of New Orleans.

Darcy Lou jumped at the chance to help her mother with these deliveries. Now Darcy Lou could ride through the city streets, secretly searching for a glimpse of William.

Secretly searching for crush-boy while pretending to do something else entirely? Been there. Done that. For sure!
At the mall, especially, Miranda and I engage in all sorts of E.R. (Ethan Recon).

Then, one day it finally happened. A few weeks before her sixteenth birthday, Darcy went into the city with her mother, as usual. At one of the shops, Tallulah had to discuss a list

Cool. Sounds like Digital Bean with outdoor seating

"Café au lait"—coffee with milk. I wonder if they served smoothies there, too?

of rush orders with the florist, so she told Darcy Lou to take a long walk.

Darcy strolled around Jackson Square for a while, and then she saw the cheerful green-and-white-striped awning of Café du Monde, an open-air pavilion where customers sat at small tables, sipping cafés au lait and eating warm beignets.

Darcy took a table. And while she waited for her order, she heard a familiar drawl coming from just behind her.

"I really hate to admit this," the masculine voice said, "but it's truly a relief to get out of that place!"

It's him! Darcy Lou thought. William Chatelaine at last!

Darcy felt her pulse racing, her breath quickening, her palms sweating. She turned in her chair, ever so slightly and ever so carefully, and glimpsed his handsome, raven-haired profile. He had just sat down with a redheaded boy, about the same age. Both wore their blue school blazers, dark ties, and gray slacks.

When the redheaded young man glanced

over at her, Darcy Lou quickly turned away.

"So you didn't like any of the girls at the garden party?" asked William's friend.

"They're all the same, Jackson," said William.

William's friend, Jackson, laughed. "Well, of course, they're all the same. They're girls. They live their lives in a desperate effort to conform."

Hey! I'd be really angry at that sexist remark . . . if it weren't . . . sort of . . . well, true. . . .

"I wouldn't laugh too hard," said William. "Except for our hair color, you and I look like a pair of twins, don't we?"

Yeah, that's right! Boys want to conform, too!

"I didn't mean it like that," said Jackson. "I mean girls think it's *important* to dress alike, act alike, whereas boys just do it to get by."

"How do you know girls don't just conform to get by, too?" asked William.

Good point

"Because they . . . " The boy's voice trailed off.

"Yes?" prompted William. "Can't you think of a reason?"

"Oh, I don't know, William. I just think you expect too much."

"I just want a girl who's got a mind of her

own. A girl who has something to say. These New Orleans debutantes my mother wants me to court all say the same things, think the same things. Most of them just parrot back what I say. They're a bore."

Wow, these boys are really quick. I think Gordo is about the only boy at Hillridge Junior High who could hold his own in a conversation like this one. Most of the other boys at school would probably be suggesting a belching contest about now.

"But they're very pretty bores," said Jackson.

"Pretty is as pretty does," said William.

"Aren't you deep."

"You know, Jackson," William told his friend, "the most interesting girl I met in the past year wasn't a debutante at all."

"Oh, really. What is she, then? A waitress here at the café?" Jackson started to laugh.

"Actually, she's a girl I met in the bayou," said William.

Darcy Lou stopped breathing the moment she heard those words. She sat so still, she thought her heart might actually forget to beat.

"The bayou!" cried Jackson. "What in heaven's name were you doing in the Louisiana swamps?"

"Getting a pair of alligators to hunt me," said William.

Darcy Lou had to slap a hand over her mouth to stifle a burst of laughter.

"William, I think you got too much sun at that garden party."

"No, really," said William. "Now that I think about it, that girl was the most fascinating young woman I've ever met."

How sweet!

"Well, your mother wouldn't be too happy to hear her future daughter-in-law spends her spare time alligator hunting," said Jackson.

William laughed. "I don't know. It sounds like a tempting idea."

"They'd throw you to the alligators for sure."

"Yes, I suppose they would."

"You, my friend, had better try harder. Your parents are going to want to see you engaged by the time you go to college. And that's less than a year away."

"I'm trying," said William. "But I think I've already been introduced to every eligible girl in New Orleans. Twice. And I'm just not interested. . . ."

What about Darcy Lou! Darcy Lou's eligible, you idiot! And you just called her the most fascinating young woman you'd ever met!

"I know. I know," said Jackson. "They're

all a bore. Hey! I just thought of something. I've got your problem solved."

"You do?"

"The Gold Mask Ball at Mardi Gras," said Jackson. "Ever been to it?"

"No," said William.

"Well, you're going this year, my friend," said Jackson. "Debs from all over the South come to that ball. New blood."

"Really?" said William. "That does sound interesting."

"I promise you, William, if you go to that ball, you'll meet a girl who will knock your socks off."

"Okay, okay," said William. "I'm willing to try just about anything at this point. You're on, my friend. The Gold Mask Ball, it is."

"Here you are, miss!" announced the waiter so suddenly Darcy Lou nearly squeaked in surprise.

On her small café table, the waiter placed a café au lait and an order of beignets. The sweet fried dough was drowning in powdered sugar, and Darcy forgot the first rule of beignet eating. She allowed a sudden intake of breath right before a big bite. The powdered sugar went right up her nose, and a fit of coughing suddenly overcame her, causing the perfect gentleman, William Chatelaine, to turn around in his chair and ask, "Miss? Are you all right?"

Darcy Lou sat frozen still as a statue.

"Miss?" he asked again.

"Yes, thank you," Darcy finally said, forcing her voice up two octaves so there was no chance he'd recognize it.

A few minutes later, when she heard the boys deep in conversation once more, she took the opportunity to place some money on the table and slip quietly away.

Oh, wow. That reminds me of the time Miranda told me this stupid joke at the 5th Grade Art Fair, and I got nose milk right in front of Parker McKenzie's sand painting. I turned her realistic portrait of the Statue of Liberty into an abstract mess. I don't think she ever got over it. (That and my sitting on her Titanic lunch box in 3rd grade.)

The next few weeks flew by, and before Darcy Lou knew it, her sixteenth birthday had finally arrived.

As usual, the Orchids and Gumbo Poker Club assembled around the Beignets' big mahogany dining room table. Also, as usual, a pot of seafood gumbo and a fresh sweet potato pie were presented to Darcy Lou.

With her usual loving care, Tallulah placed

sixteen candles into the pie and, one by one, lit each of them.

Suddenly, Darcy Lou turned to her *Tante* Dalphia, the crazy aunt who read palms and sold Cajun remedies and voodoo potions to wealthy women in New Orleans. "When I blow out my candles this year," said Darcy Lou, "will you make your incantation like you used to?"

"Oh, yes!" cried Dalphia, overjoyed that Darcy Lou had decided to make wishes again.

For the past two years, Darcy had told Dalphia that she shouldn't bother with her incantation—that since she now knew all about her father, she didn't have any more birthday wishes to make.

This had made the Orchids and Gumbo Poker Club rather sad. They had enjoyed helping Darcy Lou's wishes come true, and they all felt somewhat guilty that they'd had a hand in getting Darcy into trouble at school. They all wanted to make it up to Darcy, but none of them knew exactly how.

"I do have a wish this year," Darcy Lou said.

So Dalphia waggled her bejeweled fingers and said, "Make a wish, make a wish, while the smoke's still here, and it will take your wish to heaven, dear."

Darcy Lou closed her eyes, blew out the candles, then announced in a loud, clear voice, "I'm sixteen today, and I've never been kissed. And I wish more than anything in the world, to have William Chatelaine give me my first kiss—at the Gold Mask Ball!"

Sweet sixteen and never been kissed! (Hey, girl, what about Gator! I bet he'd help you out!)

The Orchids and Gumbo Poker Club let out a collective gasp. Then, after a good long minute to consider it, the aunts looked at one another and smiled—because they all knew one thing: if any four women on earth could make Darcy Lou's wish come true, *they* could.

THIS I gotta see!

Chapter 5
Lulubelle of the Ball

"NOW TELL ME, DARCY LOU," said Tallulah, "are you *sure* about this boy? Who *is* he, anyway?"

Whoa. Sounds like the grilling I got when my parents found out I was dating our paperboy, Ronny. Mom took it okay, but Dad was so bent, he was, like, totally ready to cancel home delivery.

Darcy Lou was about to answer, but Maribelle spoke up first. "William is from a very influential family," she told Tallulah. "I should know. Doesn't his last name ring any bells?"

"Chatelaine . . . Chatelaine," murmured Tallulah. "Oh, yes! Of course! You were nanny to that family, weren't you?"

"For eight years. And these past two years, William's been driving down here to the bayou to wish me a happy birthday," said Maribelle. "That's how Darcy Lou happened to meet him. The first year, I was present for their little encounter. The second year, I just *watched* them from my kitchen window."

Oh! That is just like a nosy grown-up to spy on you and not even inform you that you were being spied on! (Not that we don't spy on grown-ups, but that's different.)

"You were *watching*?" asked Darcy Lou, amazed her aunt Maribelle had never mentioned a thing about it in all these months.

"Oh, yes," said Maribelle. "Don't you forget, Darcy Lou—in the bayou, there are no secrets."

"William Chatelaine comes from a very fine family, doesn't he, Maribelle?" asked jolly *Tante* Jo-Jo.

"He does, indeed," said Maribelle.

"A very rich family, too," added crazy *Tante* Dalphia.

"That's right," said Maribelle. "They have money, influence, pedigree, and history. None of which Darcy Lou possesses."

That's kind of harsh! I don't possess any of those things, either—especially a pedigree (and who knew people had pedigrees? I thought pedigrees were just for poodles and terriers and stuff. . . .).

Darcy hung her head.

"But Darcy Lou has *other* blessings," said Tallulah, taking her daughter's hand and squeezing it tight.

"Indeed she does," said Maribelle. "And if

she wants a kiss from Mr. William Chatelaine—at the Gold Mask Ball, no less!—well, then, she's going to need them."

"Does that mean you'll help me?" Darcy Lou asked hopefully.

"Of course, we will!" Tallulah cried, glancing at each one of her three closest friends. "*All* of us will help you. Because if my little sweet potato likes a boy . . . well, I say it's that *boy* who's the lucky one!"

GO, Tallulah!

Most of the time, that's really how I feel about my mom, too . . . like when she chaperoned our science camping trip, and took the blame for leading the girls' tent on a TP raid to get even with the boys for Super Soaking us. How many moms would do that? And how many would give up a perfectly good lipstick so their daughter's classmates could have war paint? Yeah, sometimes my mom really rocks.

"Oh, thank you, Mama," said Darcy Lou, her heart soaring. "I'm the luckiest girl in the world to have a mama like you!"

For the next few months, the Orchids and Gumbo Poker Club put aside their weekly card game. Instead, the four women concentrated on another sort of gamble: preparing Darcy Lou for the Gold Mask Ball.

"No, no, no! Your head must be held up at all times," Maribelle told Darcy Lou during one Sunday's deportment lesson. Mirabelle taught at *Miss Charlotte's Ballet, Tap, and Charm School,* so she knew exactly how to instruct Darcy.

"Only young ladies of class and elegance are in attendance at the Gold Mask Ball," continued Maribelle, "and I assure you that none of them will be staring at the floor, looking for cans to kick!"

Whoops. I sort of do that, now that I think about it! (I mean, I don't look for cans to kick. But I do look at the floor when I get nervous.)

"I'm trying!" insisted Darcy Lou. "But these high heels are murder!"

"You must learn to glide, Darcy Lou," said Maribelle. "No matter *what* your footwear!"

"Sweet potato, try thinking of yourself as an egret or royal tern," suggested Tallulah. "You've seen how elegantly they fly? Just pretend you have wings and you're gliding above the bayou."

"Oh, yes!" said Darcy Lou. "I can do that."

"Now go to the end of the room and try again," commanded Maribelle. "Lift your chin. Good. Don't forget to open up from neck to waist. Keep your head up and push your torso forward. Very good! Again!"

After the lessons in deportment, including how to enter and exit a room, as well as sit like a lady, Darcy Lou had to learn how to properly converse.

ARRGGHH! I've been walking and sitting since I was one! I'd go absolutely nuclear if someone made me take lessons in it!

"You're a well-spoken girl, but you have to

be careful with your grammar," said Maribelle. "You've read enough books to know what is correct and what is not."

"Yeah," said Darcy Lou.

Maribelle raised an eyebrow.

"I mean, *yes*, *Tante* Maribelle."

"Good," said Maribelle. "Now the prevailing wisdom taught at most charm schools these days is to instruct girls to be agreeable."

"Agreeable?" asked Darcy Lou.

"Yes. Never argue with your date. Better yet, if you already know what topics interest your young man, then you must learn as much as you can about those subjects so you might converse intelligently with him. Now, I believe Master William is learning how to improve his game of golf—"

"No," said Tallulah suddenly.

"No?" asked Maribelle.

"My Darcy Lou has a mind of her own," Tallulah told Maribelle, "and that's the way it should stay." Then Tallulah turned to Darcy Lou. "If you spoke to William twice, then you already know how to speak with him, don't you?"

Ugh. Golf again. Reminds me of the time I tried to learn all about golf so I could talk with Ethan Craft. I bought the magazines, watched a video, swung a club or two. WHAT a boring game. And did I get a bite from Mr. Craft? Let's just say I missed the putt, big time.

Darcy Lou shrugged. "I guess so."

"Then you just go on speaking to him—about whatever interests *you*. Otherwise, you'll probably just bore yourself to sleep—which means you'll bore the young man himself to death," said Tallulah. "Let's move on to waltzing lessons, if you please, Maribelle."

Good advice—but there are exceptions. Once I saw Kate at the Digital Bean, talking to one of the swim team guys after practice. She talked nonstop about what interested her, all right: day spas, French manicures, shoes, herself—the guy's head hit the table so hard, I thought he'd have a concussion!

"If you insist, Tallulah," Maribelle said with a little smile, as if she secretly agreed with Tallulah, after all.

In a few weeks, Darcy Lou was waltzing like a dream, and before she knew it, Christmas had come and gone. Quick as a wink, it was Twelfth Night—January 6, the "twelfth night" after Christmas—and the official kickoff date of the Mardi Gras carnival season.

As many as forty balls would be held throughout the city in the six weeks between Twelfth Night and Ash Wednesday. Only a few of those balls were very exclusive high society gatherings. And the Gold Mask Ball was one of them.

"The ball is by invitation only," Maribelle said during a January Orchids and Gumbo

Poker Club gathering. "And I have no idea how we're going to get Darcy Lou in."

"I do," said Dalphia in a loud, clear voice. It was the *first* time she'd offered any suggestions during all the months of Darcy Lou's preparations. "The fact is, I've been working on it for some time now," she added, then gave a crazy little laugh and ran her bejeweled fingers through her long, gray-streaked hair.

"What have you been up to, Dalphia?" asked Jo-Jo.

"It's a fine plan," said Dalphia defensively. Then she turned to Darcy Lou. "My dear, are you willing to go along with what I say?"

"Oh, yes!" said Darcy Lou. "Anything that will get me into that ball."

"Then listen carefully," said Dalphia. "I tell fortunes for many wealthy clients in the Garden District. And I've already started a rumor about the mysterious young lady with golden hair who'll be attending the Gold Mask Ball."

"Me?" Darcy Lou couldn't believe her ears.

"Oh, yes!" said Dalphia. "I've told them

this mysterious young lady, who will be wearing the Mardi Gras colors of green, gold, and purple, will bring good fortune to any young man who dances with her."

Oh, good rumor! That one's right up there with "Kate has an aunt who's an L.A. Lakers cheerleader."

"Oh, my goodness! And they believed you?!"

"Of course," said Dalphia with a crazy cackle. "They're as superstitious as they come. But, Darcy Lou, you will never be admitted as yourself. You must attend as a special guest. So we need to come up with another identity."

"Argyle," said Maribelle.

"Argyle?" asked Darcy Lou. "As in socks?"

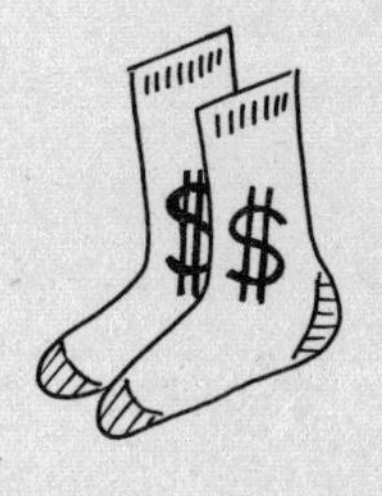

"Yes," said Maribelle. "The Argyle family of Mobile is very wealthy. It's quite believable that one of the young heiresses of that family might be in attendance at a New Orleans Mardi Gras ball."

"What's her first name, then?" asked Tallulah.

"Lulubelle," said Dalphia. "I always liked that name."

"Lulubelle," repeated Darcy Lou. "I like it, too!"

"But how will we get her on the guest list?" asked Maribelle.

"You leave that to me," said Dalphia. "One of my best clients is a sister to a member of the Gold Mask Ball committee. A little whisper in her ear and a pinch of potion in her punch will easily get Lulubelle's name on the guest list. Don't you worry, dear—come hell or high water, the Orchids and Gumbo Poker Club will make your sweet-sixteen birthday wish come true!"

Wish I could get the recipe for that potion! I can think of a few people I'd like to make vulnerable to persuasion! Ethan Craft, for one!

Finally, the big night came. All the aunts came to the house that Saturday afternoon to help Darcy Lou get ready.

Using satin and lace scraps from her dressmaking jobs, and photos from French magazines, Jo-Jo had sewn Darcy Lou a gorgeous ball gown. She'd created something truly original in the Mardi Gras colors of purple, green, and gold. No other girl at the ball would have a dress that looked anything like it!

Okay—purple signifies justice; green signifies faith; gold signifies power. The colors were selected back in 1872 when a Russian duke named Alexis Romanoff came to New Orleans during Mardi Gras. The upper crust gave a parade for the duke and adopted his household colors. The tradition stuck. (I am so ready to write my book report!)

Jo-Jo had also made a gold half-mask for Darcy, which would cover her eyes and nose.

She'd started with cardboard, covered it in hand-embroidered gold fabric, and adorned the edges with beautiful feathers, which Darcy herself had collected along the bayou's banks.

"How do I look?" asked Darcy Lou, twirling in her just-finished gown. Below the formfitting bodice, a petticoat with layers of lacy tiers made the gown's colorful skirt pouf out like a brilliant bell. The V neckline, adorned with lace, showed off her trim figure and cream-colored neck and shoulders.

Lulubelle . . .
supermodel!

"Beautiful!" cried Jo-Jo.

"Oh, sweet potato," said Tallulah. "I just can't believe my little girl looks so grown up!"

"I cut out some photos of hairstyles from the French magazines, too," said Jo-Jo, "so we can do Darcy Lou's hair up like a princess."

"What do you think, Maribelle?" asked Tallulah.

Maribelle was frowning.

"Something wrong with the gown?" asked Jo-Jo.

"Of course not. It's gorgeous. But she still needs gloves," said Maribelle.

"Oh! I've got them," said Jo-Jo. "I just

finished them last night!" She handed Darcy a pair of long golden gloves that perfectly matched the gold of her dress and mask.

"And . . . " said Maribelle. "There's something else missing. . . . "

"What?" asked Darcy Lou.

"Jewels," said Maribelle. "I'm sorry, but that V neckline leaves you as naked as Eve herself. Every other girl at the ball will be wearing jewels around her neck and a diamond tiara in her hair." Maribelle sighed. "What shall we do?"

Jewels! No way. The closest thing to a "jewel" in my possession has been a CD of her latest hits. I guess it would be nice to have expensive jewelry. But I know what Gordo would say: "Lizzie, what matters is being a good person. It's not about the bling-bling!"

"None of us has jewels," said Jo-Jo sadly.

"I know," said Maribelle. "But it *is* a must."

Suddenly, Tallulah ran out the French doors and into the back garden.

"Mama?" Darcy Lou called after Tallulah. She was sure her mother had run away to cry, and Darcy Lou felt terrible about it.

But Tallulah hadn't run away to cry. She'd run out to her garden to bring something back.

"I have the solution right here," said Tallulah, holding up a dozen orchids.

"Yes, I see what you have in mind, Tallulah," said Maribelle. "And I do think it will work. Yes, I think it will work just fine!"

While Jo-Jo worked on putting up Darcy Lou's hair, Tallulah created the adornments for her daughter's neck and head.

No jewels were needed now because Darcy Lou's mother had clipped her rarest and most prized orchids. Then, using all her skills—along with a good bit of florist wire—she molded them first into a breathtaking necklace of blossoms and then a tiara of flowers.

Awwww . . . That's so awesome! Mom's prize orchids are better than bling-bling any day!

"I've wrapped damp pieces of cotton around the stems with florist tape," Tallulah told Darcy, "so my orchids will stay fresh for hours."

Nice tip! Thank you, Martha Stewart!

"Oh, Mama!" cried Darcy Lou with tears in her eyes. "You've cut your rarest orchids. Your most prized blossoms!"

"No, Darcy Lou," said Tallulah, hugging her daughter close. "Don't you know that there's no more valuable and rare flower in this home than you? And now you're ready, sweet potato. You're finally ready to become the belle of the ball."

"Don't you mean the Lulubelle of the ball, Mama?" said Darcy Lou with a laugh. Then she kissed her mother's cheek and waltzed out the French doors, toward Maribelle's parked car.

"Don't forget, Darcy Lou," said Tallulah, "twelve midnight."

"I'll be here, Mama."

"So will we," said Tallulah.

The entire Orchids and Gumbo Poker Club had driven into the city to deliver Darcy Lou to the Gold Mask Ball.

When they reached the Hôtel du Monde, Maribelle drove her old Ford sedan past the front entrance and around to the side of the grand hotel.

"Come on out, honey," said Jo-Jo as she opened Darcy Lou's door. Darcy stepped out onto the wide sidewalk, and Jo-Jo helped refluff her skirt.

How do you fluff a skirt?! Wow, petticoats must have been a real pain!

"Remember, wait for a large group," said Mirabelle.

"I know! Don't worry!" said Darcy, even though her own nerves were beginning to prey upon her.

"You have the time of your life, sweet potato," said Tallulah.

And Darcy Lou was off, gliding along the sidewalk on her high heels. When she turned the corner, she saw a big black limousine pulling up to the hotel's red carpet. A party of three women in floor-length ball gowns and four men in white tie and black tails were exiting the vehicle. All of them were wearing gold masks.

"It's now or never," Darcy Lou murmured and swept in right behind them as they climbed the marble staircase and passed through the carved white columns that flanked the entrance to the hotel.

Good thinking! Actually, that's sort of what I try to do every day at school. When in doubt, just act like you belong! (And, for heaven's sake, don't trip!)

Darcy Lou tried not to gape as she entered the Hôtel du Monde's lush lobby. Magnificent chandeliers sparkled high overhead, and French Impressionist artwork lined the corridors. She marveled at the pink marble fireplace, which had been modeled after the one in the Grand Hôtel in Paris.

When she reached the huge archway of the grand ballroom, she saw a line waiting to descend the great staircase, down to the crowded ballroom floor. As Darcy waited, she had to keep telling herself not to look down, bite her lip, or fidget with her gown and gloves. Finally, she herself got to the top of the staircase.

"Good evening, miss," said a gentleman in what looked like a fancy doorman's uniform. "Invitation, please."

Darcy Lou's stomach clenched. Every guest in front of her had presented his or her engraved invitation to the doorman, after which the doorman had turned to the room and announced the guest's arrival.

You know, this whole thing reminds me of the time Miranda, Gordo, Matt, and I tried to sneak onto the set of a Christmas-themed music video being shot in our hometown. The only thing that saved us from jail time was Matt's bringing along elf costumes so we could look like the extras. (One of the few times my criminally insane little brother turned out to be helpful. One of the very few times!)

"I am Miss Lulubelle Argyle of Mobile," said Darcy, just the way Dalphia had told her, "and I am on the committee's special guest list."

"Yes, miss," said the man. He turned to a bearded gentleman sitting at a table nearby. "Lulubelle Argyle. Special guest?" asked the doorman.

The bearded gentleman consulted the long list in front of him. Slowly he nodded his head, and then he smiled at Darcy Lou. He actually *smiled* at her!

"Lulubelle Argyle of Mobile!" the doorman then announced to the entire ballroom. "Special guest!"

Two hundred gold-masked faces turned upward to look at Darcy Lou. Four hundred pairs of eyes, curious, critical, and ready to judge.

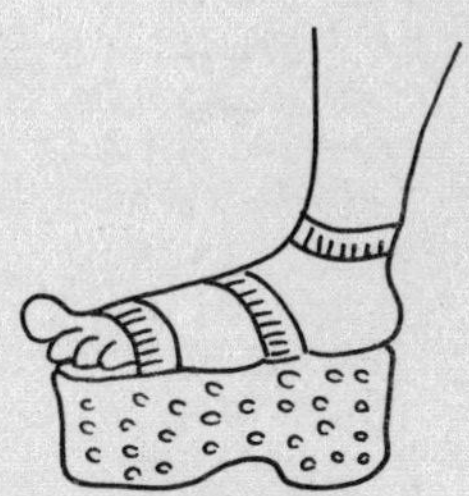

Hmmm . . .
I wonder if
visualization
exercises will
work when I'm
running for class
in my super-
stacked corkies!
Worth a try!

Swallowing her frightful nervousness, Darcy Lou just kept repeating her lessons. She pictured the beautiful birds of the bayou, descending regally toward the water, as she took her first step forward.

Eventually, she made it all the way down the grand staircase on her high heels without tripping over her cloud of petticoats. She was in!

Now what? she wondered.

But she didn't have to wonder long. A large group of young men quickly gathered around her at the bottom of the staircase.

"Good evening," she said to them.

The group seemed to hesitate collectively; then one young man stepped up behind her. "How do you do this fine evening, Miss Argyle?" he drawled.

Nice self-control for a masked ball, but, frankly, spinning like a top is pretty much required in the halls of Hillridge if you want to avoid unidentified flying objects (like spitballs, Frisbees, paper airplanes, and—if it's a food-fight day—pretty much anything on the cafeteria menu).

Darcy Lou resisted the urge to spin like a top. Instead, she remembered her lessons and turned gracefully.

"Quite fine, thank you," said Darcy Lou. "And what is your name, sir?"

"Jackson Bentley," said the redheaded young man. "At your service, miss."

It was Jackson! Darcy Lou realized. She recognized his voice as that of William's friend from the café, the very person who'd urged William to come to tonight's ball.

"Would you by any chance know if Mr. William Chatelaine is in attendance this evening?" asked Darcy Lou as primly as one of Maribelle's best charm school students.

"Why, yes, he is, miss," said Jackson. "In fact, he's a good friend of mine, and he just watched you arrive with a great deal of curiosity."

"Would you mind introducing me?" asked Darcy Lou.

With a smile of triumph, Jackson offered his arm in front of the other young men. "This way, miss."

Darcy Lou felt her heart racing as Jackson

presented her to William. Like everyone else, he wore a gold half-mask, but Darcy Lou had daydreamed so much about him, she recognized his jawline, his raven hair, his tall, lanky form the very moment they approached. Darcy Lou would have known William Chatelaine anywhere!

Darcy Lou held her breath. Would he recognize her, too?

"Good evening, Mr. Chatelaine," drawled Darcy Lou.

"Miss Argyle," said William, gazing into her eyes. "I'm enchanted."

She nearly swooned when he gallantly bowed over her gloved hand.

Ohhhh! How romantic!

Come on, Darcy Lou, she told herself. The Orchids and Gumbo Poker Club worked for months to make this moment happen for you. Don't let them down now. Pull yourself together and show the boy you're not just some little shrinking violet!

"The pleasure, sir, is mine," Darcy managed to respond ever so coolly.

"And what brings you all the way from Mobile this fine evening?" asked William.

Darcy Lou paused a moment. "Well, if you want to know the truth, it's a very serious matter." She gestured for William and Jackson to lean in close. "The truth is," she told them in a hushed tone, "our Red Cross division heard you New Orleans boys were bored sick with all the young women in Louisiana. So they sent me on over to see what I could do."

Ha!
Good one,
Darcy!

You go, girl!

Jackson burst out laughing. William just stared.

"What's the matter, Mr. Chatelaine?" Darcy asked. "Cat got your tongue?"

"Oh, he'll recover," Jackson teased. "He's just never heard a girl as pretty as you express anything resembling wit in all his born days."

Suddenly, the orchestra struck up a waltz, and William found his voice.

"Miss Argyle, would you care to dance?" he asked, offering his arm.

"Oh, yes, Mr. Chatelaine. I'd love to," said Darcy Lou. And dance they did. For the next few hours, William never left her side, and, despite her high heels, she felt as if she were dancing on a cloud!

They laughed and talked all evening. Finally, William fetched two glasses of punch. Then he offered his arm and took her to a secluded section of the ballroom, where a balcony allowed them to see Mardi Gras fireworks in the distance.

After the fireworks were over, they gazed at the stars overhead.

"Orchid girl," teased William, "I think you are the most charming young woman I have ever had the pleasure of meeting."

Darcy could hardly believe it. There weren't just stars in the sky tonight—there were stars in William's eyes . . . for her!

Keep your head, she told herself, hearing Maribelle's advice. Don't show him you're ready to swoon—even if you are!

"I'll wager you've met quite a few," said Darcy Lou, coolly sipping her punch.

"What? Girls?" asked William.

"No," teased Darcy Lou. "Brown pelicans."

"Funny you should mention brown pelicans. I saw one just last fall," said William. "It's the state bird of Louisiana, you know."

Darcy nearly laughed out loud. "Is it?"

Uhm, hello! She knows! She told you that, you doofus!!

"Being a girl from Mobile, I wouldn't think you'd know that," said William.

For some time, Darcy Lou had wondered if William had the least little idea that he had met her before. By now, however, she was convinced that he had absolutely no idea he'd been dancing all night with the "Alligator Chicken" girl.

Darcy Lou was very tempted to take off her mask at that very moment and remind him. Very tempted, indeed! But she didn't dare risk doing anything that might end this marvelous dream, burst this wonderful bubble.

And, besides, there was one last thing Darcy Lou had wished for that had not yet come true.

"I've often mused how a bird's life is not unlike our own," said Darcy. "Full of flights and perchings."

"Is that so?" said William. "And what are you looking for tonight, may I ask? A flight? Or a perch?"

"I don't know, Mr. Chatelaine," said Darcy Lou. "I think this bird is still making up her mind."

"Well," said William, "perhaps this bird can be persuaded?"

"And how, pray tell, do you propose to do that?" she asked.

Slowly, William's green eyes met her blue ones, and then it happened. He kissed her!

At last, THE KISS!!!!!! 'Bout time!!

Darcy Lou couldn't believe it. She thought she had died and gone to heaven. In the distance, one last Roman candle shot up into the night, blooming across the starry sky like a blossom of light.

Ohmigosh!! I just hope you didn't need a mint, Darcy Lou!

(Oh, well . . . I guess in stories, everything's always perfect at moments like this. I mean, Cinderella never worried about halitosis, right?)

Finally, the kiss ended. The orchestra struck up again, and she felt William taking her hand.

"Let's dance all night!" he said with a smile as wide as the Mississippi.

She was about to agree when she heard the clock in the church bell tower across the square striking midnight.

No, no, no! Darcy Lou wailed to herself. The dream can't be over. It can't be! Not yet!

Dang! She's on Cinderella time, all right!

But it was, and Darcy knew it.

Tallulah and the Orchids and Gumbo

No fancy carriage? Bummer! Cinderella leaves the ball of her dreams, and all she finds for a ride is three soccer moms in a lame family car.

Poker Club would all be waiting for her around the corner in Maribelle's old Ford sedan. She couldn't keep them waiting—not after all they'd done to make her birthday wish come true.

"If you'll just excuse me," Darcy Lou told William. "I have to . . . " Her voice trailed off. She didn't know how to tell him she had to go.

"Oh! Of course," said William, misunderstanding. "Let me escort you to the powder room."

That's right, William—when ya gotta go, ya gotta go!!

When they reached the ladies' room door, he said, "I'll wait for you by the punch bowl."

Darcy Lou hated leaving William like this, but she didn't know what else to do. So, the moment his black tails were out of sight, Darcy slipped through the service exit and out into the dark alley, leaving the splendor of the Gold Mask Ball to fade behind her like the last brilliant shimmers of fireworks light.

"Oh, Mama, it was the most wonderful, magical night of my life!" Darcy Lou exclaimed when she finally arrived back home. "And the best part about it was that it wasn't *imagined* at all. It was well and truly *lived*. It was *real*!"

"It *was* real, my darling, but it was also imagined," said Tallulah, sitting with her daughter on the veranda swing. "Make no mistake, you had to imagine it before you could make it come to be. You'll find that everything in life is like that, Darcy Lou. Never forget."

"I won't. And I'll never forget one more thing."

"What's that, sugar?"

"This night never could have happened if *you* hadn't imagined it with me, Mama, if you hadn't cared what I wanted most and convinced your friends to help me make it come true."

"Oh, sweet potato," said Tallulah, "don't you know the secret sisterhood of all mothers?"

"What sisterhood is that? Do you mean the Orchids and Gumbo Poker Club?" asked Darcy Lou.

"Yes, sugar. I do. And more. I mean the

sisterhood of all mothers—in every place and every time. We all want our daughters to be happy, and to have everything their hearts desire. All we mothers are the same in this wish for our daughters, I promise you."

"Oh, Mama, I love you," said Darcy Lou. "And I'll never forget this night you helped give me!"

"I love you, too, sweet potato!"

Smiling to herself, Darcy Lou lit a candle and headed up the dark staircase. A part of her wished the ball could have gone on forever. But she well knew she'd masked more than her face tonight, and she didn't dare hope for more than her one perfect kiss. Reaching for more would have been like trying to keep a snowflake from melting, a soap bubble from popping.

Throwing open her bedroom window, Darcy Lou breathed in the heavy, sweet air of the bayou night and wiped away a single tear. One last long look up was all she wanted. For it was there, in the heavens, that she'd be able to recapture the very same feeling she'd had on that hotel balcony.

Ohmigosh . . . I actually think I'm going to cry, too. . . .

Darcy Lou quietly removed her gloves, set them on the divan, and blew out the candle. After that, there was only night, and stars, and the memory of love.

It's so beautiful!

Chapter 6
Lost and Found

"WHAT DO YOU MEAN, YOU don't have an address or phone number listed for Lulubelle Argyle?" asked William Chatelaine, the morning after the Gold Mask Ball. "Please look up her name again."

Check it out, Prince Charming needs a universal Yellow Pages!

"I'm sorry, Mr. Chatelaine," said the woman from the Masked Ball committee on the other end of the line, "but she's merely listed as a 'friend of the committee.'"

"Yes, I see. Well, what name from the committee is given?" asked William. "Who sponsored her?"

"There's no name listed," said the woman.

"But *somebody* had to have sponsored her," said William, unable to believe his ears. "No one gets into the Gold Mask Ball without a sponsor!"

"My good young man, I know the rules as well as anyone. The Argyles are an influential Mobile family. Clearly, they pulled some strings to get Miss Argyle into the ball—strings which the family doesn't even wish *us* to know about."

"Why, in heaven's name?" asked William. "Why all the secrecy?"

"I dare say the family was trying to discourage young men from tracking that beauty down to pester her after the ball—just as *you* are trying to do right now, Mr. Chatelaine. My advice to you, young man, is this: if Miss Argyle did not see fit to give you her address or phone number at the ball, then I suggest you resist the urge to pursue her any further. Good day."

William could not believe his ears. The woman had hung up on him! He called around to everyone he knew—but no one had ever met Miss Lulubelle Argyle before, even

DISSED! Ouch! That's gotta hurt!

though many had heard about her coming to the ball.

Argyle family tree (Yes, we have no Lulubelles!)

William attempted to contact the Argyle family next, but they treated him as if he were some sort of crazy stalker. One gentleman even claimed he'd heard of no Lulubelle in the entire Argyle family tree!

It was his friend Jackson who came up with the idea of tracing the orchids.

"There are only so many flower shops in New Orleans, William," said Jackson. "Why don't you inquire around. I guarantee, the florist who made that tiara of rare orchids is bound to remember the girl who wore it!"

But William had no luck at all. None of the florists, not one, said they had made a tiara of orchids. Not *ever*.

"As far as orchids go," said one florist, "we deal in single and double corsages only."

"Then, where would someone get that many orchids?" asked William, completely frustrated. "Where would they have had a necklace and tiara made?"

The great orchid detective!

"The girl might have hired our supplier directly," said the florist.

He's getting warm. . .

"And who is your supplier?" asked William.

"A woman named Tallulah," said the florist. "I can give you her address, but I warn you, she lives over an hour's hard drive outside the city. Down in Bayou Le Blanc."

He's getting warmer!

He's red-hot now!

"So, do ya love William Chatelaine, Darcy Lou?"

Darcy Lou nearly fell out of Gator's wooden pirogue. The two of them were floating in the middle of the bayou swamps, fishing in total silence. That question of Gator's was the last one she had ever expected him to ask her, especially since he'd been against her Gold Mask Ball plan from the start.

"I don't know," said Darcy Lou. "I mean, I do feel something for William . . . but I've convinced myself that it's best to put him out of my mind. . . . I mean, I don't see any point in prolonging something that can never be . . . I mean, I don't feel comfortable discussing it with you, Gator."

"Well, why the heck not?" said Gator. "You told me all 'bout going to the ball, didn't ya? Even though I hated the idea of your tryin' to pretend to be somebody else. Plumb crazy . . . Darcy, ya know, ya can talk to me, don'tcha? We're best friends, aren't we?"

"Yes, we are," said Darcy Lou.

"Ya know, girl, ya might've improved your diction and gotten lessons in waltzing, but you're still the same ol' Darcy Lou inside. I'll be able to see through any mask you might put on for the world, ya know. 'Cause we're best friends. That's what counts, right?" asked Gator.

"Yes, it is," said Darcy Lou. "It sure is . . . but my feelings for William . . . they're confusing . . . and they're private. And, if you don't mind, sometimes a person might want to keep her feelings private."

"Oh, I don't mind," said Gator. "You know, I got private feelings for someone, too."

"You do?" Darcy asked. "A girl?"

"Of course. I'm not about to fall in love with no alligator, Darcy."

"I didn't mean . . . I just meant . . . I'm *surprised,* that's all. You never mentioned anyone."

Wow. This Gator dude really does remind me of Gordo . . . not that Gordo ever said "plumb crazy" in his entire life. But he's always saying how it's more important to be a good person and a good friend, to be real, than to spend your life totally stressing about whether you're wearing the latest style or whether the "in" people are saying you're cool or not. . . .

The truth is, Gordo's his own man . . . a one-of-a-kind guy. . . . In fact, when I think about it, Gordo really is the coolest guy I know. . . . In his own way, I have to admit, he's even cooler than Ethan Craft. . . .

Darcy Lou waited for Gator to tell her more, but he didn't. Finally, she couldn't stand it anymore. "Who is she?"

"Well, I'll tell ya, Darcy Lou, it's like you said. Sometimes a person might want to keep his feelings private."

"Oh, of course," said Darcy Lou, feeling strangely all of a sudden that Gator might have feelings for another girl. But why should she feel strangely?

Ohmigosh!! Darcy thinks Gator likes another girl . . . but it's, like, totally obvious he likes HER!

Gator was just a friend . . . wasn't he?

Geez, some girls are really slow on the uptake!

"Oh, my goodness!" Darcy Lou cried when she approached her house that afternoon.

Get a clue, Darcy Lou!

The little red convertible sports car was driving up—not to the front of Maribelle's house, but to her own.

"Excuse me, miss," said William, as he climbed out of the car. "I'm looking for a woman named Tallulah?"

Excuse ME, you idiot! Like, open your eyes!

Darcy Lou stood stock-still. Her hair was in a ratty ponytail, her slate-gray cotton jumper splashed with bayou water.

"Miss?" prompted William.

"What do you want with Tallulah?" asked

Darcy Lou. Her wide blue eyes were staring right into William's green gaze, and he still hadn't recognized her. For some reason, this made Darcy Lou's blood begin a slow boil.

"I want to know—" William suddenly paused. "Excuse me, but don't I know you?"

Hello, Prince DUH! She's your Cinderella!

"You should, William Chatelaine," said Darcy Lou in a scolding voice. "You should."

"Oh, no," said William. "You? You . . . you can't be . . . "

"No," said Darcy Lou, "I can't. So, shove off."

Darcy Lou started for the house, unwilling to explain herself in any way to William. But he wasn't letting her go that easy.

"Wait!" he cried, catching hold of her hand. "Wait."

"Why?" Darcy Lou turned to face him, but she didn't want to. She was furious.

"You're the one," said William, his voice still incredulous. "You're Lulubelle Argyle—"

ABOUT TIME, FELLA!

"Try Darcy Lou Beignet," snapped Darcy.

"It doesn't matter what your name is. I fell in love with you last night," said William. "Whoever you are, I love you."

NOW YOU'RE TALKING!

For the next few weeks, Darcy Lou thought she was the happiest girl who ever walked the face of the earth.

William Chatelaine, the boy she'd dreamed about for ages, had just declared his love for her!

She'd said she loved him, too, of course, and a whirlwind courtship quickly began after that. Darcy Lou immediately introduced William to her mother. When Gator stopped by, she told him the happy news, too. He said he was happy for her—but then he'd left abruptly without another word, and she'd been too busy to see him much after that.

Oh, wow, that must have been so hard for Gator!

Darcy Lou was flying so high, she barely noticed anything. William was taking her out on the town almost every night. And then, it finally happened—Darcy Lou was asked to meet William's family!

The dinner was difficult for Darcy. The

OOOOOh! Do I hear wedding bells?

(Sigh)

Mrs. Ethan Craft

Mrs. Lizzie Craft

Mrs. McGuire-Craft

family wasn't very friendly. It all seemed very stiff and formal, but she was sure it had gone well enough. Unfortunately, William confided that his family had many reservations about his seeing Darcy Lou. They wouldn't yet allow William to formally propose marriage to her, and he told her that outright.

You tell him, girl! He's got nerve!

"But *you're* the one who wants to marry me. Not them," said Darcy Lou. "How can they stop you?"

"They're my family," William explained. "When you marry me, you marry them, too."

"I don't understand," said Darcy Lou. "You said you loved me."

"I do. But—"

Well, I think Darcy's right. And I bet Gordo would agree! (After all, when it comes to friendship, there shouldn't be any buts, either.)

"When it comes to love," said Darcy, "there shouldn't be any buts."

"But sometimes there are," said William. "You'll just have to help me persuade them to give their consent, that's all. Try harder to win them over."

"How?" asked Darcy.

"We're having a garden party this Saturday," said William. "Why don't you bring your family. Maybe that will help."

"There's just my mother, really," said Darcy Lou. "My grandfather is bedridden. And my father . . ."

"Yes?" asked William. "You never want to talk about him. Is he away on business?"

"My father died in the war," said Darcy Lou, suddenly uncomfortable about saying anything more.

Ah, yes . . . I remember. Ben Terpen and the Hatbox Talk.

Darcy Lou invited her mother to the Chatelaines' garden party. But from the moment they arrived, Darcy knew she was in trouble.

The Chatelaine garden party wasn't a masked ball, and she was no longer pretending to be an Argyle heiress. No masks now. Nothing to hide her identity as a girl from the bayou backwoods.

William's sister and cousins looked her up and down with a collective sneer. And William's mother did the exact same thing to Tallulah.

"Who are your people, Mrs. Beignet?" asked Mrs. Chatelaine.

"My *people*?" said Tallulah. "Well, we've been farmers and fishermen, mostly. The bayou

Kinda reminds me of Kate trying to pretend she's not a year older than the rest of us because she was held back in kindergarten. (I'd still like to know how you get held back in kindergarten: whaddya do—fail milk and cookies? Get an incomplete in nap time?) Well, anyway, we all found out.

Mom says our people were Polish immigrants (Mom's side) and midwestern farmers (Dad's side). Not exactly "descendants of the *Mayflower*" material . . . but, hey, at least we're not snobs.

I remember when Matt thought our real family history wasn't impressive enough and he had to do a presentation to his class, so he said we were descendants of George Washington, Davy Crockett, and (if you can believe it) Elvis. I'd have to say that was a tad extreme—even for Toad Boy.

is a beautiful place to live. And I grow orchids for almost all of the New Orleans florists—"

"You should see her garden," said Darcy Lou. "It's the most beautiful garden in all of Louisiana."

"A gardener, yes," said Mrs. Chatelaine. "We have a hired gardener ourselves. He comes twice a week." Then she rudely turned from Darcy and Tallulah and walked straight over to William. Her words did not appear to be pleasant ones.

After the party, William drove Darcy and Tallulah back to the bayou. Tallulah went inside, and William asked Darcy Lou to stay behind.

"We need to talk," he said.

"I don't like the sound of that," said Darcy Lou.

ARRGHHHH! "We need to talk" is what Ronny said right before he dumped me! To quote my mom: "Nothing good EVER follows 'We need to talk.'"

"My mother thinks you're a charming girl. But . . ."

"But?"

"But in the future," said William, "it would be better if your mother didn't come with you to our social gatherings."

"What?" Darcy Lou felt as though he'd

He wants Darcy to dis her own mother? EX-SQUEEZE ME?! That is totally bogus! He can't be serious!

just pulled out a knife and stabbed her through the heart.

"It's not so bad, Darcy Lou. It's important that you understand you're moving up in the world. You took an awful lot of trouble to get into the Gold Mask Ball, didn't you? I mean, you *do* want to be a part of my world, right? And if you want to be a part of it, you must learn the rules."

THIS IS SO NOT COOL!

"Birds of a feather flock together. Is that what you're saying?" asked Darcy Lou tightly, her fists clenching.

"That's right."

"Well, William, if you're telling me I can take it or leave it, then I choose to leave it. And you!"

You go, girl!!!

Darcy climbed out of her passenger seat and slammed the car door so hard, the whole vehicle shook.

"Just think about it, honey—"

"I don't need to. And I'm not your honey. And, frankly, after a good hard look at your stuffy, boring, judgmental world, you can have it. I'll take life here any day, thank you very much!"

You've just been christened Titanic, dweeb boy.

Get ready to SWIM!

For some reason, Darcy Lou suddenly flashed back on that time in the school cafeteria when Adele Aleman had insulted her and Gator had stood up to defend her.

Back then, Gator had told Darcy Lou that *watching* a friend being hurt or rejected was far worse than experiencing it yourself.

Darcy Lou finally understood Gator Guidry. She might have been able to overlook an insult to herself, but not to her mother. Never to her mother.

After William drove off, Darcy Lou ran to see Gator. She hadn't talked to him in weeks, and she suddenly missed him terribly.

"Gator's gone," said his mother when Darcy Lou knocked on his screen door.

"Gone?" Darcy Lou couldn't believe it. "Gone where, Mrs. Guidry?" she asked.

"Didn't he tell you, Darcy Lou?" asked Mrs. Guidry.

"Tell me? Tell me what?"

"We're all so excited for him. A teacher at school helped him take some test that got him an early entrance to a special college. It seems he's a whiz at botany. They say he's a prodigy!" cried Mrs. Guidry.

"College! Where?"

"California. He's long gone, Darcy Lou, honey. I'm sorry, but he's long gone."

Code Blue!
Code Blue!
How could Gator
Do that to her?

Ohmigosh! I'd be so totally ruined if Gordo did that to me. He'd never leave me like that. Not even a good-bye . . . would he?

Chapter 7
New Horizon

A YEAR PASSED, EACH OF ITS twelve months as slow moving to Darcy Lou as the dankest section of the bayou swamp.

Go straight to completely miserable—do not stop at somewhat sad. . . .

After graduating high school in May, Darcy Lou spent all of June helping her mother tend to and sell her orchids. Darcy loved her mother dearly, but there was something missing in her life. Darcy just didn't want to admit it. And with Gator gone off to college, Darcy didn't even have her best friend to confide in anymore.

I'd totally shrivel up and die if Gordo did this to me. . . .

"I want you to do something for me, Darcy

Of course, Darcy did sort of leave him first, didn't she . . . ? Hmmm . . . food for thought.

Lou," Tallulah finally said, one day late in the summer.

"What's that, Mama?" asked Darcy Lou.

"I want you to leave Bayou Le Blanc."

"What?" asked Darcy Lou. She couldn't believe her ears.

"You heard me," said Tallulah.

"But, Mama!"

"You must find a life for yourself, Darcy Lou. A life that makes you happy—"

"But I'm happy here," insisted Darcy Lou.

This is so sad! I mean, Tallulah loves her daughter so much, she's actually willing to be miserable herself and have Darcy leave home just so Darcy will be happy. . . . (I think I'm going to cry again. . . .)

"You're hiding here, sweet potato, like a muskrat under a log. And I won't watch you waste the best years of your life. You have your father's imagination. You have his gifts. And I'm not about to stand by and watch you squander them. I love you too much, sweet potato."

"But, Mama, what will I do . . . ? Where will I go?"

Tallulah handed Darcy Lou a clipping from a recent newspaper. "Your *Tante* Maribelle showed me this. I think you should see it, too."

Darcy Lou read the clipping. It was a

contest for a scholarship to a college in another part of the state.

"You just have to write a short story, Darcy Lou," said Tallulah. "And if there's anything my girl can do, it's tell a story!"

Darcy Lou did write a story. And by early August, she found out she'd won the scholarship. A week before she was preparing to begin classes for the school's fall session, she heard a knock on the frame of the screen door.

GATOR'S BACK!

"Hey there, Darcy," called Gator Guidry. "You interested in a little boat ride?"

AWESOME!

"Gator!" Darcy raced to the veranda and hugged him tightly. When she let go and took a longer look at him, she was amazed at his transformation.

Gone were his raggedy overalls and overgrown hair. He now wore pleated, belted pants with a knife-sharp crease, a snow-white shirt, a silk tie, and even a snappy blue blazer. And his sandy brown hair was trimmed short and brushed back. With his tall, strapping form, Darcy Lou decided he looked about as good as any young man could!

Hey, dude! Looks like your Rodeo Drive makeover worked!

Now Gator's DEELISH!

After Gator said his hellos to Tallulah, he

shed his jacket and tie, and took Darcy by the hand, pulling her out to his old pirogue.

"I want to show you something," said Gator. "I think you'll like it."

He turned off to a section of swamp she hadn't been to in years. Using the oars to guide the boat, he pushed in near a cluster of very old, very big oak trees.

"Look," said Gator. "Wild orchids."

Sure enough, there was a cluster of beautiful orchids growing right there at the base of the trunks.

"I heard about your breaking things off with William Chatelaine," said Gator. "I also heard about your scholarship. And I wanted to come back to visit you before you started college. I would have come sooner, but my botany professor took me with him on an expedition to the Brazilian rain forest. Well, today's *our* expedition. And before you leave, I'd like to show you something to always remember our friendship by."

"Oh, Gator," said Darcy Lou. "Just seeing *you* again is enough."

"You mean that?" asked Gator.

"Of course, I do," said Darcy Lou. "I've missed you this past year. You've always been my very best friend. It's been so hard without you."

"I'll always be your best friend, too, Darcy," said Gator softly. "Always."

"Gator . . . "

"Yes?"

"I *do* need you," said Darcy Lou. "I truly do."

Darcy Lou looked into Gator's eyes and smiled.

"Do you love me, Darcy Lou?" Gator dared to ask.

"I do, Gator," said Darcy. "I know that now more than ever. I do love you."

"Then, I have a question for you," said Gator. He reached outside the boat, picked one of the wild orchids, and wrapped its stem around Darcy's left ring finger. "Will you marry me, Darcy Lou Beignet?"

I am totally crying again!

"Oh, Gator! Are you sure?"

"I've always been sure," said Gator. "It's you who's been the big question mark."

"Oh, Gator, I'm not a big question mark

anymore. I *know* what I want. I want you in my life. Always!"

'BOUT TIME, GIRLFRIEND!

Then Darcy Lou threw her arms around Gator and kissed him so long, she reckoned it just might have made the *Guinness Book of World Records*.

Darcy Lou and Gator agreed to get married after they finished college. Four long years they waited. Gator transferred to a school closer to home, and after they had both earned their degrees, they tied the knot for good.

The day of their wedding, Gator got the good news he was waiting for. The botany professor for whom he had begun working received funding for an expedition to the Galápagos Islands.

Where in the heck are the Galápagos Islands? Mr. Dig? You sub for geography, too, don't you? Give me a clue! And, PLEASE, don't tell me to look it up. I've looked up ENOUGH stuff in this book already!

"That takes care of the honeymoon," Gator told his new wife. "We've got to get packed and onto a ship in three days."

Tallulah, Maribelle, Jo-Jo, and Dalphia all helped Darcy Lou get ready for the trip. Jo-Jo even cooked up a big feast for their goodbye party. It would be at least a year, maybe more, before Darcy Lou even saw Tallulah again, and Darcy Lou felt her heart growing sadder and sadder as the day for good-byes approached.

Finally, the time came. Gator was waiting out front in the car, and Darcy Lou went inside to give her mother one last hug.

Tallulah was on the veranda, with a look on her face like a bayou cloudburst. Darcy Lou watched her through the French doors, like staring into a thousand futures.

"Mama? I'm fixin' to go now, Mama," said Darcy Lou.

"Before you go, Darcy Lou," said Tallulah. "I . . . I . . . I want you to have this. . . ." Tallulah handed Darcy Lou a small box.

Darcy remembered this box. She'd seen it once before—when Tallulah had revealed to Darcy Lou who her father really was.

"Oh, Mama," said Darcy Lou, as she opened the box to look inside. "It's the bracelet Ben Terpen gave you!" Darcy couldn't believe it. She knew how much this bracelet meant to her mother! "Why are you giving it to me, Mama?"

I wish my mom would give me a bracelet filled with special meaning for her. . . .

"Oh, sugar," said Tallulah, "wherever you

go, well, that's where my heart and soul have to be. And when I die and sink beneath the bayou mud, part of me will always be with you."

With tears in her eyes, Darcy Lou ran to Tallulah and threw herself into her mother's arms. "Oh, Mama, Mama. I want us to be friends! Friends forever."

"Oh, I'm so glad, sweet potato," said Tallulah. "And I can finally say it—welcome to the Orchids and Gumbo Poker Club."

"Oh, Mama. Oh, it's good to be here, Mama. It is *so* good to be here," said Darcy Lou; then she kissed her mother one last time.

Someday, Darcy Lou would return to her beloved home. Until then, she knew she'd just have to carry its memory, along with the deep love for her dear mother, safely in her heart. And that's just what she did as she headed right through the front door and into that bright new horizon called the future.

Tallulah and Darcy love each other so much. . . . It must be so hard for both of them. . . .

I never thought about it before, but it'll be so sad for my mom when I get married and have to leave her behind. . . . It'll be sad for me, too. I'll so totally miss her. . . .

I totally can't stop crying!

Ohmigosh, I want me and my mom to be friends forever, too! I want us to start our own Orchids and Gumbo Poker Club!

I'm gonna ask her right now!

Here I come, Tallulah!

About the Author

MAGNOLIA PRALINE was born and raised in Louisiana. When she was ten years old, her New Orleans home burned to the ground during an unfortunate Fourth of July weenie-roasting incident. Magnolia then migrated with her mother and younger brother to the home of her mother's family, sweet potato farmers who lived along a bayou in southern Louisiana.

Largely autobiographical, *The Orchids and Gumbo Poker Club* was written by Magnolia when she was still in college. After college, she married a botanist who had also been a childhood sweetheart. She traveled the world with him in search of rare flowers.

Magnolia eventually returned with her husband to the southern Louisiana bayous where she wrote poetry and painted alligators in the style of the French Impressionists.

She became the mother of six and the grandmother of nine before passing away in the early 1990s. Her last request was to be buried in her mother's treasured bracelet and her favorite alligator shoes.

MALL

ETHAN CRAFT